ABOUT THE BOOK

Six spicy stories from one of erotica's hottest authors to keep you aroused and turning just one more page for hours!

No matter your kink, Janessa has you covered: the mind-blowing carnal lust between these pages will keep you coming back for more, again and again.

Include the following sultry stories:

UNDER HER BOSS'S DESK

BIG GIRL FOR THE BILLIONAIRE ROCKSTAR

CLUB LUXURIA

TRUE LIVES OF MILITARY WIVES

TAKEN RAW

WHEN DADDY'S AWAY: Older Man Younger Virgin Woman Romance

SIX SEXY TABOO TALES

EROTIC STORIES OF SEDUCTION, SEX, AND
SUBMISSION

JANESSA DAVENPORT

EUR

CONTENTS

1

UNDER HER BOSS'S DESK

Robert was just settling down at his desk, a fresh cup of coffee comfortably clutched in his hand when Karenna barged into his office, slamming the door behind her and collapsing into the chair opposite him.

"Ow!" Robert stuck his coffee-stung finger into his mouth, savoring the life-giving brown fluid despite the cruel bite of his burn. He set the cup aside at his desk and focused his attention on Karenna, hunched over, head in her hands, a halo of strawberry-blonde hair around her.

"Is your hand okay? I'm so sorry, it's my stupid fault for startling you." Tears streamed down her face, her big green eyes shot through with red. "I can't do anything right today, apparently." Somehow she still looked beautiful through her suffering, but Robert hated to see her that way.

"What's the matter, Karenna? Come on, whatever it is can't be that bad." This was no way to start off their Monday morning. They had a long week ahead of them, including a long-awaited meeting with important foreign clients. If they were able to bring this deal off, Senault Industries stood to more than double its earnings over the next quarter--and both Robert and Karenna stood to make a great deal of money. This time next year, either or both of them could be sitting in the big boardroom with all the rich old men who made the real decisions at Senault...but for that to happen, everything that week had to go perfectly.

"Ohh...it's nothing, really. I just..." Karenna glanced back at the door. "We've known each other a long time, right?"

"Um, sure...I mean, you've worked here, what--three years, two and a half under me? Yeah, I'd say that's a while."

"No, I mean..." She lowered her voice. "We can trust each other, yeah?"

Robert suddenly felt as though the temperature in the room shot up a couple of degrees. "Well, sure, Karenna, I trust you. And I'd like to think you can trust me."

"I do, Robert, I trust you. It's just, well..." She looked around furtively. "I need to get something off my chest, but it's not exactly 'office-appropriate' conversation, if you know what I mean. And the last thing either of us need this week is to get derailed by Bonnie from HR pulling us into her office for one of her lectures, you know?"

Robert nodded. "I get you. Here--the door doesn't lock, but if it'll make you more comfortable, I'll turn the radio on, so anyone who might be listening in will just hear classic rock."

Karenna smiled. "I'm sorry about all this, I know what a crazy week we have ahead of us. But if I don't get this out, I won't be able to think about anything else all day--and I can't afford to be half-assed about my performance, this week of all weeks. And, well..." Tears began to well in her eyes. "You're the only one who might understand, but since you're my boss, I didn't know if..."

"Hey, hey, Karenna, it's okay. Don't cry." He leaned over

the desk and embraced her awkwardly, patting her back and handing her a tissue. "I'm not just your boss--I'm your co-worker, and I'm your friend. Don't worry about it."

"You're so sweet." She wiped her eyes, blew her nose loudly into the tissue, and smiled despite herself. "I knew you'd understand."

"So what's the problem, chum?" Robert grimaced at his words; he was trying to keep the tone light, but he'd erred too far in the wrong direction.

"Well, it's...Joe and I have been having some...problems lately. See, we've been trying to have a baby for a long time now--over a year and a half--and it's starting to feel like, I don't know..."

"Like what?"

"Well, I guess I'm starting to feel like it's never going to happen. And worse, I'm starting to wonder if, wonder if..." She trailed off, her eyes brimming with tears.

"Oh, honey, what is it?"

"I'm starting to feel like Joe isn't even attracted to me!" She burst into tears; Robert came around from behind the desk and took her into his arms comfortingly.

"Hey, hey Karenna, don't do that, it's okay, it's okay..."

"Are you...are you sure?"

"Sure, hey, come on. I mean, look at yourself--any man that wasn't attracted to you would have to be either gay, or dead."

Holding her in his arms, looking at the reflection of her curves pressing up against him in the mirror on the opposite wall, Robert wasn't lying: Karenna had a body that was the envy of most of the office, males and females alike. He didn't know much about Karenna's husband Joe, but if he wasn't taking advantage of sleeping next to a woman like Karenna, well...it was a damn shame, that's all.

"That's nice of you to say, Robert, but...well, like this morning, for example? Last night Joe and I had a big fight right before bed...I mean, a real screaming match, neighbors-calling-the-police knock down drag out fight for the ages type of thing."

"Ouch."

"Yeah. No fun. But you know how it is, we all have them now and then, sometimes you just have to clear the air, let it all out, and then move on. It's just the way things go sometimes, right? So this morning, I wake up a half-hour early and I'm feeling...well, the best part of fighting is the making up afterwards, right?"

"Sure, yeah." Robert felt a drop of sweat break on his brow.

"So I decide I'm going to give Joe a, um...a special morning wake up." She blushed. "You know what I mean."

"I get you."

"So I start in doing my thing, and after a couple minutes I can tell he's awake...but, I mean, like, that's all. Like, he's awake, but he's not...his, um, thing isn't..."

"Oof. Yeah."

"So I keep working at it and working at it, trying to get things going, but it's just...not happening. Finally, after ten minutes--god, it felt like an eternity--he just sighs, gets out of bed and goes and gets in the shower." She turned to look at Robert, her eyes tear-filled pools of despair. "I just don't know what to do now! I just wanted to give my husband pleasure. And now, damn it, I..."

"What is it, honey?"

"Now I'm all fucking horny, and I feel like shit. I mean, really, I can't even give my husband a blowjob? What's wrong with me?" She collapsed against Robert's chest, sobbing into his lapel.

He pulled her tighter to him, feeling her breasts straining against the conservative dress she'd squeezed herself into. It wasn't right for her to feel this way about herself; from what he'd learned working alongside her, Karenna was a wonderful person, as well as being far and away the best-looking woman in the office. And on top of it, she worked twice as hard as anyone else--because with her looks, she knew if she didn't, she'd be resented by everyone. As a result, she wasn't universally loved within the office--but she was respected by all.

"Listen, Karenna...I don't know much about your...much about Joe, but I can't imagine whatever's going on with him is your fault."

"Y-you think?"

"No. I mean, maybe he's dealing with something he hasn't shared with you, or doesn't want to, for whatever reason...it doesn't make it right, but you just never really know what another person is dealing with--sometimes not even when you live with them."

"I guess so...but I'm his wife, you know? I'm just tired of being treated like, I don't know...like I'm not even a person." Karenna looked up into Robert's eyes, her pupils dilated as her eyelids rimmed with tears. "Do you know how that feels, for someone to act like you're not even there?"

Robert put his hand on the back of her head, holding her tightly to his shoulder. "There, there, Karenna. You're a person to me, and to everyone else in this office, if nothing else. And if Joe's too blind to see that, well...it's him we should feel sorry for."

She sniffed, burying her face in Robert's chest as she sobbed. "Oh, god, I'm so embarrassed. Here I'm supposed to be professional and I just come in here and fall apart on you first thing Monday morning." She broke their embrace, taking a tissue from his desk and dabbing at her eyes. "It's all so meaningless when you get down to it."

"Yeah, I know what you mean. It's easy to get caught up in the day-to-day troubles of our daily lives, and when you look around, nothing is really that big a deal when you break it down."

Karenna looked confused, then thoughtful. "Hmm, I suppose that's true...that wasn't exactly what I was getting at, but when you put it that way, I guess you have a point."

"Exactly! Come on, none of these problems are insoluble! We just have to look at them step by step as we would any other business problem, and take the most logical, efficient route to alleviate the issue. That's what Senault pays us to do, so let's do it--only for your benefit instead of the company's. Then once we've solved your problems, it's back to work. Sound good?"

Karenna smiled. "Sounds like a plan. Hmm...well, I guess the first thing to do is identify the problem." Her cheeks flushed red suddenly, and she turned away from Robert, suddenly aware of herself.

"What was it, Karenna? Something jumped into your mind just then, I could tell."

"Haha, no getting anything past you, is there?" She bit her lip nervously. "It's just, it's a silly little thing really..."

"Hey, hey. Nothing's silly here. If this is what's bothering you, this is what we need to work on right now. If it's for the good of Karenna, it's for the good of the company, after all. Right?"

"W-well..." She looked over at Robert from under her brow, then sighed and took a breath. "Like I say, I know it's silly, but...well, I didn't have any older sisters, and my family was always a little, um, repressed...so I wasn't allowed to go to sleepovers and such, and always felt like I was, well, missing out on some of what the other girls learned growing up."

"I get you. I missed a whole summer of baseball the year I had a broken leg, and I never caught up to the other guys after that."

"Right, that sort of thing. You fall behind, it's hard to catch up...and all of a sudden, you feel like it's too late to ask anyone to help or teach you. S-so..."

"Go ahead, Karenna, I'm right here to help you."

"W-well, the thing is...no one ever taught me how to um, go...down on a guy. You know." Her face blushed bright red; Robert felt more sweat break out on his brow, but he struggled to maintain his composure as she continued. "Anyway, I didn't used to feel so self-conscious about it but this morning, when Joe pushed me off him, that brought it all flooding back--and when that happens, it doesn't matter where I am or what I'm doing, I suddenly feel like that insecure little girl whose overprotective parents kept her away from everything in the world for way too long, and everything seems overwhelming and scary, and it's all more than I can handle."

"So..."

"So, well, now that we break it down, I'm realizing the problem isn't necessarily my skill or lack of same--if Joe's the problem, then I don't have to feel so shitty about myself all the time."

"Okay. So how do we find out if Joe's the problem for sure or not?"

"Well, I don't know how we test that, to be honest--I'm his wife, I know him better than anyone, and I don't have a clue. Plus he refuses to even talk about seeing a therapist, he won't even stop by and see the counselor here at work." Her eyes flashed beneath her long lashes. "But we can test the other thing."

"The...other thing?"

"You can tell me whether or not my blowjobs are any good."

Suddenly, Robert felt his head swimming; sure he'd fantasized about Karenna's lips wrapped around his cock, he'd even pictured her on her knees right under that very desk, her tongue caressing his swollen dick as he slid in and out of her ruby-red lips--but in his experience fantasy and reality were two very different things. Yet here she was, looking up at him in desperation, her big green eyes filled with need--and his cock was already rising in anticipation. He felt her eyes drift down to his crotch, then back to his face, awaiting his reply.

"Karenna, I'd love to, but...I'm your boss. I don't know if it'd be appropriate." His eyes jumped to the cheap office door without even a flimsy lock to keep it from popping open whenever anyone felt like popping in. Damn the higher ups and their 'open door policy.'"

Karenna looked up at him seductively. "Oh, come on, Robert. You've got to help me out here--you're the only man whose opinion I can really trust. And it's *because* you're my boss I'm asking you--after all, you're used to evaluating my work and providing feedback." She stepped closer to him, grabbed his tie, and pulled his head down to her, whispering in his ear. "I promise--no one but us ever has to know."

Karenna released Robert's tie suddenly and shoved him backwards with all the strength in her body; his arms flailed momentarily in alarm, but he relaxed as he sank comfortingly into his office chair. Karenna smirked down at him sprawled in the luxurious high-backed leather chair.

"Caught you off balance there for a second, didn't I?" She stepped in front of him and kneeled before him, looking up into Robert's wide eyes. "You just go about your day as usual. Meanwhile, I'll just be down here--also taking care of business." She wedged herself into the space beneath the desk, folding her long, sensual legs beneath her, only a hint of her heels protruding from beneath to betray her presence.

Above, Robert was unable to believe what was happening. *I should stop this right now, I could lose my job, we could both lose our jobs--how did I let this get so far so quickly? I need to do something now before it's too late!*

Clearing his throat, Robert started talking to the empty air in front of him, hoping the woman below him at eye level with his crotch was willing to be reasonable.

"Listen--Karenna. This is all very flattering, and I'd like to help you out, bu--"

Robert stopped short, his speech interrupted midsyllable as he felt Karenna's hand dance its way up his pants, finding the zipper. Her voice projected up from beneath the desk: "Sorry, what was that? I didn't quite catch what you said, I was in the middle of something."

"A-ahem. I, uh, was just saying that I don't know if we--"

Zzzzzip went the crotch of his pants, and Robert felt Karenna's delicate fingers push past the flap of his boxers, finding his penis and extracting him through his fly, dangling free beneath the desk. Looking down under the desk at her, he saw her staring at his prodigious cock, still flaccid but impressive even in that state--and he was getting very aroused, very fast.

She licked her lips sensuously and gazed up at him, "Oh my, boss--I never knew you were so endowed."

He smiled down, all thoughts of protest eradicated from his mind. "Where do you think my confidence comes from?"

"Oh, I always figured you didn't have anything to be ashamed of." She grinned. "But let's see if we can't do something about that."

Leaning forward, she took just the tip of Robert's cock into her warm mouth, holding it there on her tongue, savoring the taste of Robert's salty precum as she thrilled to her core, aroused and excited beyond belief at the feel of another man's penis inside her body for the first time in years. She relished the sensation of his pulsing dick rising to her touch, getting bigger and harder with each beat of his heart, pushing deeper into her mouth even as she remained still.

Adjusting herself, she pushed her head down onto Robert's now-erect cock, feeling him touch the back of her throat; he groaned above her and sank deeper into his chair and she glowed inside, knowing her loving oral caresses were pleasing the man she respected so much.

Suddenly, the door slammed open behind her and she heard a boisterous voice: "Rob! My man! My man on a Monday morning! How the hell are ya, Rob my man!"

Karenna felt Robert's cock tense in her mouth; she didn't release him, only pulled her legs beneath her and tightened her lips around his cock, still sunk so satisfyingly into her throat.

"J-Jason!" She heard Robert answer above her, his voice straining as he tried to maintain composure. "G-good to see you, dude-b-but I'm, uh, really busy this morning..."

"I get you, my man. Rough weekend? Need some of the hair of the dog that bit you?"

"No, really, I--"

"Tell you what, my dad always said the best hangover cure was the love of a good woman. 'Course he didn't mean 'love' exactly, but you get the idea."

Robert grimaced at Jason; beneath him, Karenna continued apace as if nothing had changed, sliding his cock silently in and out of her warm, luscious mouth, steadily taking his full length down her throat, holding it there momentarily as her esophageal muscles twinged, then releasing him until the bulge of his cockhead hit the back of her lips--only to repeat the motion, her pace steadily increasing.

"Well, Jason, I'll certainly take that into consideration, but like I say--"

"Anyway! Before I forget the reason I popped in here in the first place--where's that Karenna?"

Robert tensed; below him, Karenna froze, Robert's dick held between her lips.

"K-Karenna?"

"You know: legs for days, boobs out to here? Hottest piece of ass in the office?"

"Jason, that's not a--ow!--an appropriate way to talk about a co-worker."

Jason cocked his head at Robert. "You okay there, boss?"

"S-sure, sure--just, uh, pulled a muscle on my run this morning."

"Ouch! No fun. So anyway, to clarify: you haven't seen Karenna then?"

"Er, not yet. Why?"

"Oh, well, someone said they saw her heading this way-- so I figured she was heading to your office. Maybe I can head her off at the pass coming back from the bathroom later." He winked at Robert and patted his breast pocket. "Won two tickets to the tractor pull from the radio, thought I'd see if she wants to go--and then see if she wants to pull my tractor later, if you follow me."

"Jason, I--ow!--Jason, I won't tell you again to maintain

proper office decorum where your co-workers are concerned. Now please exit my office--and, uh, close the door behind you."

His face crestfallen with disappointment, Jason meekly backed out of the office; the second she heard the door shut, Karenna apologized: "Sorry, sorry! I didn't mean to, it was just a reflex--that jerk was pissing me off. I'm so sick of his dumb jokes and flirting."

"Well, I think that may have taken care of it. And if it didn't, I'll see to it he never bothers you again." He caressed the side of her face lovingly. "Okay?"

She smiled, her worries assuaged. "Okay. So as long as we're taking a break, how about a midpoint performance evaluation?"

"Oh god, baby--I don't know what to tell you. I never had a blowjob so amazing in my life."

"R-really?"

"Really. In fact, I have to admit--the reason I sent Jason out of here so quickly was I was afraid I was going to come in your mouth right here on the spot. And if that had happened, there's no way I would have been able to keep a straight face."

"So, my husband..."

He shrugged. "I don't know what to tell you. I mean, sure, people have different tastes, everyone is different and likes different things, and all that. But there isn't a guy in the world who wouldn't get off of what you were doing to me down there. It was like a goddamn miracle, honestly-- practically as soon as you started, it was all I could do to hold my cum in, usually it takes me a lot longer. But your mouth, so soft, so wet..." He looked at her pillowy lips and wanted more than anything to lean down and kiss them; shaking his head, he tried to reassert his professionalism--

as much as he could with his dick still hanging out, anyway.

Tears welled in her eyes. "Th-that's great to hear..."

"Hey, hey--what's the matter now?"

"Oh, it's stupid...but I thought if I was just, you know, somehow just shitty at giving head then maybe that was what was irritating Joe. But if my oral skills really are that good..."

"Trust me, baby, they are."

"W-well, I guess it's good to know it's not me. But if that's the case, t-then...t-then..."

"Then what, Karenna?"

She burst into tears. "Then he's *never* going to give me a baby!" She collapsed forward, sobbing into Richard's crotch, her tears mixing with the sweat and precum dripping onto the seat's shiny surface. He caressed her head comfortingly, but felt his dick twitch again with arousal at the feel of her soft cheek and hair brushing against his still highly-aroused member.

Suddenly, Karenna stopped short, raised her head up, and wiped her eyes. "That's it." She met Robert's eyes, and he knew she had something of import to ask him, something that might change the course of both their lives--and he knew he would be able to deny this exquisite beauty crouched at his feet nothing.

"Robert, I need you to do something for me, and I don't think I can take it if you say no--so please listen to what I have to say carefully before answering."

He smiled into her luscious eyes, so recently his ultimate secret pleasure. "I swear."

"Okay. Well, the uh, the reason I was giving Joe the 'special wake-up' this morning was that this is one of my peak fertile days, and I was hoping...that is, uh..."

"You were hoping this would be the month."

"Yes! But it's been too long, and nothing I do can turn Joe around. I'm at the end of my rope, and I'm out of ideas." She bit the tip of her index fingernail. "But you--you can give me what Joe won't. What Joe can't."

"Karenna..."

"Oh please, Robert, please--please don't say no. I need this more than anything, I don't think I can take this any longer--I just need it. I need you." She stared deep into his eyes, and he saw the soul depth of her need, to be fulfilled as a woman, to achieve what she wanted most in life.

"Karenna...how could I ever say no?"

She broke into a wide grin and felt her long-dormant juices beginning to flow. "Oh god, Robert, thank you so much....you don't know how happy you've made me!" Seductively, she peeled her conservative business skirt away from her hips, revealing her already-sopping pussy through her dripping wet white panties. "But I'm going to show you. Oh, how I'm going to show you."

Slowly, Karenna slid her hands down her body, taking her panties with them, exposing her soft, wet, labia to Robert's gaze; the most beautiful he'd ever seen, he knew at once he would do anything for her, no matter what she asked. She reached down to his crotch and gripped his base firmly; his cock responded instantly to her touch, springing back to its full length and hardness. "I do like a man who shows up to work on time."

He raised his hand in a scout salute. "Perfect attendance record right here, ma'am."

"Well, showing up is half the battle," she replied. "But the other half is putting more in than the other guys. Can you do that?" She stepped one long, sensuous leg across Robert's body, straddling him in the office chair while continuing to stroke his hard member with one hand.

"I think I can promise that."

"Well, there's only one way to find out." She lowered herself onto him, his rock-hard cock sliding easily into her soft, wet pussy--at least the first few inches of it. She whimpered slightly as he pushed up against her walls; years of deprival had let her cavern withdraw, lacking the presence of a man to maintain its boundaries. Now, as he pressed into her, she felt the pain of her repression--but her passion welled within her and her nethers flooded with arousal, her wetness easing the pain, relieving the straining tissue as it stretched to contain Robert's invading member.

"Oh, my--oh my fucking god, Robert," she moaned. "You're so fucking big, I can taste you in my stomach." She pushed down onto him, forcing him deeper within her; she gasped momentarily, surprised by the depth of his intrusion, his long dick pushing against her cervix, but her torso twitched with delight as he rammed into her, pushing deeper and deeper. "Oh god, I finally feel like a fucking woman again!"

"Oh fuck, Karenna--you feel so good!"

Their eyes closed in ecstasy, neither one saw Robert's office door crack open--and neither one saw the single blue eyeball peering through the tiny crack at the two of them, Karenna riding her boss in ecstatic joy, her face radiating joy as his virile penis rammed into her over and over.

Oblivious to the eye of their onlooker, Karenna redoubled her effort, finally successfully pushing down on her boss's hard dick and containing its massive length within her; she smiled despite herself, filled and fulfilled, exultant in her womanhood.

Tightening her vaginal walls on him, she groaned her pleasure and he moaned in response.

"Oh god, baby, I'm about to...I'm gonna..."

She leaned down and put her luscious red lips against his ear, whispering--but not so quietly the observer at the door couldn't hear every word--"Do it, Robert, do it now--come in me, I want you to come in me more than anything, please come in me now!"

He strained, driving himself as deeply into her as he could; she nearly screamed at the pleasure of his hard cock so firmly lodged inside her, stretching her body in ways it had never been before, and all her vaginal muscles fired off as she came with the force of months of repression. The shockwave of sheer pleasure rippled through her body and Robert saw the joy spread across Karenna's face in the kind of smile she wouldn't be able to wipe away for hours.

Satisfied his job was done to completion, Robert relaxed a muscle he'd been keeping tightly cinched in his perineum, finally allowing himself to reach his height of pleasure. He sighed in joy as his aching scrotum gave up its load into Karenna's yearning womb, fertile ground waiting for his seed as if manna from heaven. Karenna clung to him, savoring the joy of a man's essence soaking her, knowing she wouldn't be able to continue depriving herself as she had been.

Behind them, Robert's office door silently closed. Neither Robert nor Karenna had spotted the observing blue eye--but it had definitely taken note of what they had done.

Her breath heaving from her prodigious chest, Karenna grinned down at Robert, still sunk deeply into her--though rapidly retreating from his full state of arousal--as satisfied as he could remember being. "Well boss, I think I managed to get my problems solved--and here it is not even 9AM yet!"

"See what you can accomplish when you put your mind to it?"

Grabbing a handful of tissue from Robert's desk, Karenna dismounted, gathering her clothes. "That's true--but in my experience, you can only get so far in this world without having the right people around you." She beamed at him. "I'm just lucky to have you there, just when I needed you."

"Well, Karenna, I'm glad I could help. And just so you know, I'm here for you anytime you need me." He smirked. "After all--we have an open door policy here at Senault!"

The two of them laughed, their cackles of joy penetrating the thin office door and sinking into the ear of the blue-eyed voyeur crouched just outside Robert's office door. The edges of the voyeur's mouth curled up at Robert's joke--it was a funny joke, perhaps even funnier than either of them knew.

But they'd find out. *Oh, how they'd find out.*

2

BIG GIRL FOR THE BILLIONAIRE ROCKSTAR

L iving in the same tiny Indiana town you grew up in is just as glamorous as you always heard. Mossy Grove isn't a bad place, but it can get a little stifling when everyone you see every day knows each other, along with each other's family, each other's family's history...you get the picture.

It's a quiet town for the most part, the same as a thousand little flyspeck towns around the state except for one thing: as a result of a bequest from an anonymous benefactor decades ago, Mossy Grove High School has always had an amazing music program. Sure, Mossy Grove students go nuts for sports and partying and all the other things teenagers do, but they also have more bands per capita than any other school around the state. Rock, country, metal, jazz, hip-hop...you name it, Mossy Grove High School kids played it. It was just the way things were in Mossy Grove, and people didn't think anything was all that different or special about it at the time. But as time went on, most of the students came to recognize what a golden moment they'd shared and how lucky they were to grow up in a place where music was celebrated--and making it together with fellow students was not only easy and fun, but encouraged.

The good times of high school never last forever, though, and Mossy Grove was no different from any other town in that respect. After senior year, bands tended to break up quickly as members moved away, went to college, got full-time jobs, and started families. But there were always a few that somehow managed to beat the odds, to stick it out, and keep going where all others fell by the wayside...so over time, Mossy Grove built up a reputation as the little Hoosier town that launched a music revolution. Not that much of note ever happened within the city limits, per se--but when you add up all the hit songs that former Mossy Grove students went on to make, all the devoted fans screaming at successful tours mounted by Mossy Grove graduates, and all the gold and platinum discs earned by fellow Mossy Grove alumni, it can start to get a little over-whelming.

These were the thoughts tumbling through Lorraine's head as she sat in the Mossy Grove roadside diner eating eggs, bacon, and sausage as she did every workday morning, idly browsing the day's headlines. The sad irony was that due to hearty Midwestern mealtime habits, it was almost all guys from her class that went on to fame and fortune in the music industry. At the time, all the record label scouting agents agreed that Lorraine could sing, but none of them could figure out a way to market her. Now, of course, it all looked so obvious in retrospect--but back then, it seemed more than anyone could imagine for an industry dominated by old white men to make way for one curvy girl with a voice.

So reluctantly, Lorraine had sucked up her pride, put

her ambitions on the shelf, and gone to work at the Mossy Grove Bank like many of her friends. Only rarely did she regret the way her life had gone. For the most part, she was happy with who she was: no, she might never have fulfilled her dream of singing at center stage in Carnegie Hall, but she'd also never be a size 2--and she had accepted both of those things.

Yet sitting there in her favorite diner eating her favorite breakfast on a beautiful Thursday morning, Lorraine couldn't help frowning down at the article she was reading. That weekend the 10 year reunion of her graduating class was scheduled, and the local gossip column was all abuzz about which chart-topping Mossy Grove hunks would be dropping in to make appearances. Officially, the only band scheduled to play the reunion was a local cover band stocked with fellow Mossy Grove High alumni whose most impressive achievement was rocking the Mossy Grove Tavern every Friday and Saturday night for the last two years straight. Yet somehow, everyone expected a star-studded roster of unannounced guest appearances. True, Lorraine's graduating class had given rise to some of the top performers in the country, many of whom were at the peak of their earning potential--so why would they be taking time out of their busy schedules to drop back into the craphole that spawned them?

She sighed, flipping through the gallery of pictures depicting some of the larger-than-life figures people somehow hoped to be stalking the town's streets once more that weekend: behatted country superstar Scotty Adkins, tattooed pop-metal bassist Mikky Foxx (who Lorraine still thought of as Mikey from third-period art), heartland rocker Bart J. Johnson...and then, one last picture pierced her vision and Lorraine's breath stopped.

Rick.

It still stung. Rick Bloomfield had been the guitarist in her band back when the record labels were scouting her out, when they were both still aspiring to professional music careers--and to maintain that professionalism, they had resisted their intense attraction to each other. To give him credit, Rick had stuck it out with her the longest of anyone as the band slogged it out night after night trying to build a following, replacing member after member as the scouting offers dwindled and people moved on with their lives.

But then, it all ended. Lorraine's eyes wavered as she recalled the events of that night: one minute Rick was there, packing up his equipment after yet another disappointing gig--and the next she turned around and he was gone. No note, no call, no email--nothing.

Lorraine had panicked, calling the police, the FBI, everyone she could think of--until she got in touch with Rick's parents, who calmly informed Lorraine that their son was on his way to Japan, en route to a meeting with the head of a giant multinational record company. Lorraine still recalled the feeling, standing there in a phonebooth in the rain in the middle of nowhere as the realization sank into her that she had been abandoned by her longest-standing ally in music without even so much as a word.

In the years to come, Lorraine had cringed every time the subject of Rick popped up; fortunately, since most of the population of Mossy Grove was already well aware of her history it was rarely brought up in polite conversation. But there was nothing she could do about all the times when she'd be watching television and suddenly there his face would be, playing on a talk show or accepting another award. She'd assumed the ache would heal over time, but at that moment sitting there in the diner, her teeth idly working the same cold bite of egg she'd been chewing on for three minutes, the pain felt as fresh as if it had been the day before.

Tossing her napkin onto her plate, she left a crisp $10 on the table and headed out to her waiting car. Turning out of the diner lot, the gas light began blinking and she sighed. *Ugh, it's one thing after another. Might as well fill it up now, I guess.*

She pulled into the familiar 24-hour filling station and the attendant waved her down, wiping his hands on a greasy rag. "Morning, Lorraine. We don't usually see you in here this time of day."

"Just topping off the tank, Stevie," she replied, rummaging through her purse. "All I can find is a fiver for now, but I'll be back later."

Steve grinned down through the window. "Bag's still a disaster area, huh?"

"You know, I try and try to keep my life in order, but somehow no matter what I do it always seems to get away from me."

The attendant shook his head. "Well, it ain't like you're not coming back this way, girl. Tell you what--I'll fill you up to the top here, just get me back the next time you swing through."

"Oh, thank you, thank you, Stevie! That's so sweet, I can't thank you enough."

"Ain't nothing, I know you're good for it, Lorraine." She popped her gas cap, the man stuck the nozzle into her waiting tank and she heard the reassuring rush of the liquid pumping through the long hose into her vehicle.

"Well, I know I have it in here, it's just..." She shrugged. "You think you have a handle on things, and then something comes along and turns everything upside down, and one thing piles on top of another, and then you never seem to get caught up."

"I hear ya. S'why I never left the gas station--keeps life simple as possible. True, ain't the most glamorous lifestyle, but at least I get to meet and talk to plenty of pretty ladies. And around these parts everyone still needs gas for their cars, after all--for now, anyway."

"You and your silver tongue will get through somehow, Stevie--I can't imagine an impersonal plug replacing the service you provide here at the Mossy Grove Gas N Go."

"I hope you're right, Lorraine, I surely do." The gas pump handle clicked as Lorraine's tank filled. "There you go Lorraine--and hey, look at that! Just by coincidence, it took exactly five dollars of gas to fill your tank to the top."

She smiled suspiciously at the man. "Stevie..."

"Now, Miss Lorraine, sometimes these things happen. You just hand me that five dollar bill and we'll call it even this time."

"Stevie, you'll never turn a profit this way."

"Lorraine, I ain't at any risk of turning a profit this year any more than I have been any other--and I don't see any reason to change now. " He took the crinkled bill from her outstretched hand and tucked it into the pocket of his over-alls. "Tell you what--you can buy me a drink if you see me at the reunion this weekend."

"Oh, Stevie--I don't even know if I'm going to go."

"What do you mean? Be a great chance to see everyone from the old gang again. Come on, it's gonna be a time. You have to go!"

"I just... " She lowered her eyes. "You, me, everyone who stayed around Mossy Grove--I don't have any issues with anyone here, but I get to see you guys all the time anyway. But among the people who moved away, well... there are some faces from the past I'm not as anxious to dredge up, Stevie."

"That may be as it may be, Miss Lorraine--but did you ever consider that maybe it's because those people moved away that you still have issues with them? After all, I don't recall you and me getting along any too good back in high school--you had your crowd, I had mine. But over the past ten years we've come to be more than nodding acquaintances, haven't we?"

"Of course, Stevie."

"Of course we have. And as I recall, you and Margie Lawson used to fight like cats and dogs in the 8th grade, but now you both love that book club you have together like it's the best part of your week. It ain't nothing special: it's just you run into people enough, you start to see things from their perspective, and next thing you know you're fast friends. I'm betting if you'd had a chance to talk to some of these other people who left town the way you have all us locals, those faces wouldn't be so scary."

"I don't know, Stevie--maybe you're right." She bit her lip, considering her dilemma.

Suddenly, a loud, shiny roadster came hurtling down the street, banking sharply as the driver steered the careening vehicle towards the gas station. Stevie stepped out towards the roadway, waving his arms as he guided the car to a halt.

"Hey, hey! This ain't the Indianapolis Motor Speedway, buddy!"

The mirrored windows of the car lowered, and a chagrined face peered out. "Sorry, my man--I haven't driven these roads in a while, and this thing got away from me. It's a rental, I never drove one of these before and it's taking me a little longer than I expected to get my bearings."

Stevie looked the sleek red vehicle over, his lips emitting

a low whistle. "Well, I can't say I have either, so I ain't gonna get on you too much. Powerful piece of machine you got here, though."

"Yeah, I'm told it's the top of the line."

"Must be sweet. How many miles to the gallon does it get?"

"Well it...doesn't run on gas. It's electric, actually."

Stevie's face crinkled as though he'd bitten into a lemon.

"I see. So, what can I do for you today?"

"Well, I just got into town, and I was hoping you could--Lorraine?" The motorist suddenly caught a glimpse of the woman unsuccessfully ducking her head below her window in the other lane as she tried to avoid being seen. "Lorraine Johnson, is that you?"

She sighed, abandoning her futile attempt at conceal-ment. "Hello, Rick."

"Oh, my god!" The man came leaping out of his expen-sive rented roadster and bounded across the pump island; Lorraine remained seated inside her vehicle as he approached, his jeans hugging his thighs tightly as his powerful legs strode towards her.

God, he hasn't changed a bit, she thought. If anything, he was more muscular than the last time they'd spoken. Rather than the lithe form of an underfed indie rocker, Rick now carried the weight of a man's body, his arms now bulging with the strength of many mornings spent strength training, his abs rippling underneath the tight t-shirt clinging to his frame.

Rick leaned on the edge of her open window, bending down to flash a gleaming white smile. "My god, Lorraine--it's so good to see you."

"It's--good to see you too, Rick." She couldn't help but feel self-conscious; back in the days when they'd played together, Lorraine certainly hadn't been what anyone would have called waiflike, but she'd also had the metabolism of a twenty year old. She'd also been trying to get a career in the public eye off the ground, so she'd spent every single day fighting her instincts, futilely trying to stick to whatever fad diet the latest rail-thin Hollywood starlets were pushing. None of it ever really worked, and as time went on and any hopes of a life in the public eye faded away, Lorraine had packed on weight slowly but steadily. She wasn't unhealthy, and she had grown to love herself the way she was, but she couldn't help mentally comparing her current appearance against her silhouette as it had appeared the last time she'd seen Rick.

"Listen Lorraine, I'd love to stay and chat but I'm running late for a meeting right now, unfortunately. I was just stopping in to get directions-- ever since I hit the Mossy Grove city limits my mapping app doesn't seem to be taking me where I need to be."

"Yeah, that'll happen around here. People used to complain, but the big guys have made it pretty clear they don't really care about what happens to folks way out in the boonies like us. And after all, most of us who stuck around town still know how to find our way around." She grimaced as the words exited her mouth; she hadn't meant to sound so bitter, but every word seemed soaked with venom and veiled meaning.

"Uh--well, I guess you're probably right about that." Rick looked taken aback, as if not sure whether to flee back the way he'd come. "So, um--are you going to be at the reunion tonight? To tell the truth, I was kind of hoping we could get the chance to...talk for a few minutes."

Lorraine looked at him, her eyes ablaze with pain and

suppressed passion. "I just don't think that would be a good idea, Rick."

"But...Lorraine, I just..."

"No, Rick." She turned her face away; looking into his aching dark eyes was too difficult. "It's been too long, and too much has changed."

"I haven't changed that much, Lorraine--under all the flash and glamour, I'm still the same guy you knew."

"Well then, maybe that's the problem, Rick. Because I have changed." She put her sunglasses on, hoping the dark lenses concealed the tears welling in the corners of her eyes. "It's been years and I've moved on. I don't want to dwell in the past or thoughts of what might have been. I can understand how you'd relish the opportunity to sweep back into Mossy Grove, let everyone see what a big rock star you've turned into--but that doesn't mean I have to watch it."

She turned the key in the ignition and sped off before Rick had a chance to respond. *Damn him*, she thought as tears rolled down her cheeks. *Another two minutes and I would have been down the road and on my way to work, I never would have seen Rick and his stupid flashy red car.* She wiped tears from her eyes as she checked herself in the rearview mirror. *Ugh, can't let anyone at work see I've been crying, better fix myself up before I do anything.*

She set her jaw, composed herself, and tried to force herself into the proper mindset for work, pushing all thoughts of Rick and his rock-hard torso from her head as she concentrated on the road before her.

One thing's for sure, she told herself. *No way in a million years I'm getting dragged to that stupid reunion tonight.*

TEN HOURS LATER, Lorraine sat waiting impatiently at the bar for her wine to arrive.

"Hey, how many of those have you had already tonight?"

"Don't even start with me, Andrea," Lorraine shot back as the bartender set a long-stemmed glass in front of her. "You don't know the day I've had." Besides, Andrea weighed maybe ninety pounds soaking wet and got tipsy after half a bottle of light beer, so she was the last person Lorraine needed commenting on her consumption.

"Sorry hon, didn't mean anything by it," Andrea cooed. "It's just the beginning of this magical night, after all, and it'd be a shame to miss any of it later."

Lorraine raised one eyebrow at her.

"I can handle my liquor, thank you very much, and I assure you that if I should miss anything later, it'll be due to my own choice--and not because, say, I was passed out in the bushes with Jimmy Farnsworth's hand up my skirt."

Andrea blushed bright red, turned on her heels and stomped off as Margie Lawson took the stool next to Lorraine at the bar, addressing the bartender.

"Rum and diet in a tall glass--make it a double." She sighed, turning to face Lorraine. "That Andrea, always stirring it up. At least the alumni committee sprang for the open bar."

"Hear, hear." The women clinked their glasses together and sipped. "I may have to step up from wine too if this day gets any worse," Lorraine lamented.

"What's the matter, Lor? You've been looking forward to this for months."

"I know, I just...you know how sometimes you get something set in your head the way you want it to be, and even though you know there's no correlation to reality, it's still the way you'd like it to work out? It'd just be nice if just one of those things worked out just once in my life."

Margie hugged her compassionately. "Let me guess: Rick?" She looked around. "I didn't even think he was coming--where is he?"

"Oh, he's not here yet--at least not that I know of," Lorraine sighed.

"So what's the problem, hon? You know he's got a record in the charts and a band on the road. Chances are he's far away underneath the hot lights on some stage right now, all thoughts of Mossy Grove far behind."

Lorraine shook her head. "That's what I've been telling myself, and if that man had any sense at all in his head that's exactly where he'd be. But just my stupid luck, I run into him getting gas this morning, so he's been on my mind all day." *Him and that butt of his*, she told herself.

"Oh, girl, don't let one guy ruin your night," Margie admonished her. "We've got good food, good friends, and an open bar. What's one butthead more in the mix?"

Lorraine shook her head. "Maybe you're right, Margie."

"That's the spirit! Come on, the band's just getting started--let's get our dance on before the floor fills up."

Lorraine had to admit that the beat was getting to her; the Mossy Grove Tavern All-Stars might not have been famous rock stars, but as her grandfather used to say, their playing was tighter than a mosquito's behind. The kick drum and bass made Lorraine's backside want to wiggle, and she succumbed to her friend's invitation, making her way out to the dance floor and letting her body move in glorious delight. Every beat rolled through her body as she moved with the music, her worries and concerns washing away as the guitars crashed and the keyboards tinkled around her. The few other early dancers cleared the way for

Lorraine as she danced by herself, her hands caressing her curvaceous body as the song built to a climactic crescendo, breaking down to a fierce, stomping beat as the drummer took a solo.

Sweating, the singer stepped from the stage and tapped Lorraine on the shoulder, simultaneously signaling for the bartender to bring him a beer.

"Hey, you were really getting your groove going out there!"

She blushed. "Oh, Sharkey, you know I don't usually dance that way--at least not anymore, but something about this night has me forgetting myself left and right."

He wiped his brow with one hand, accepting his pint glass with the other. "I hear you, Lorrie. We've played that tune probably a thousand times--hell, you've heard us bang it out over at the Tavern every weekend for months. But tonight..." He stared off into the distance, his eyes dim. "Tonight it was like we were...filled with the spirit. I don't know quite how else to put it."

"Well, you guys do sound great tonight."

"Thanks, Lorrie. Any chance you doing a guest spot with us later on?"

"You know I always turn you down, Sharkey."

"Oh, I know." He turned, then looked back over his shoulder. "But like you were saying...there's something about this night."

Sharkey stepped back onto the stage, taking the mic just as the drummer reached the climax of his solo. "All right! Thanks for coming out tonight, lads and lasses of the class of ten years ago--we're all mighty happy you were able to make it. My name is Sharkey and this is the Machine, other-wise known as the Mossy Grove Tavern All-Stars. We're going to be playing some songs here for you tonight--but right now we have a special guest a few of you might recognize."

Lorraine felt her heart sink to her stomach as Rick took the stage, acoustic guitar in hand. Screams pierced the air and Lorraine was caught in a crush of bodies as people rushed the little dance floor in front of the tiny stage, oblivious to the band that had been thumping away only minutes prior but suddenly enthralled by the celebrity billionaire rock star standing only feet away.

Struggling for comfort, Lorraine felt sweat break out under her arms as people crowded in around her. She couldn't help blaming them, even though she also herself felt inexorably drawn to Rick's magnetic presence as she struggled to fight her way back through the wall of bodies penning her in.

Sharkey cleared away from center stage as Rick took the mic, plugging his guitar in and clearing his throat.

"Alright! Hi, I'm Rick Bloomfield!" Lorraine covered her ears as the crowd went "WOOOOO" at the top of their lungs for thirty seconds before dying down enough for Rick to continue: "Anyway, like most of us here tonight I was born and raised right here in Mossy Grove,"--here he paused for another thirty seconds of WOOOing--"and while I've been a lot of different places since my days growing up, I've come to learn there's no place in the world quite like here."

The crowd quieted, shuffling into place as every eye and ear fixed on Rick. Lorraine stopped trying to fight her way from the dance floor, turning to watch while hoping the lights in his eyes kept Rick from seeing her.

Onstage, Rick placed a capo on the neck of his guitar, checking his tuning while continuing to speak. "Anyway, this is a song that I wrote a while ago you might recognize. It's about someone I haven't--hadn't seen for a long time.

And no matter where I am when I play it, it always makes me think of Mossy Grove...so I figured I'd play it here for you folks tonight."

The crowd roared as Rick strummed the opening chords of his chart-topping single "Preciously," a ballad that had broken out on a television drama before going on to become a slow-dance favorite at proms across the country. Around her, Lorraine could see couples sink into each other, holding hands and looking into each other's eyes as Rick angelically intoned the first lines of the song:

"As I watch you in the bedroom, dressing slowly for the night, I can hear your heartbeat beating next to mine..."

Lorraine rolled her eyes. She'd tried to avoid Rick's music, but this one had been too huge to miss--when a song gets played over the supermarket PA system, it's tough to avoid entirely. It had always struck her as saccharine and cloying when she had caught bits and pieces of the lyrics, though--not up to the standard of Rick's work when she had worked with him.

Still, it was hard to argue with success, and as Lorraine looked at the faces of the happy couples around her she felt a twinge in her soul. Her shoulders slumped, and she slowly turned to face center stage--only to find Rick staring directly at her as he went into the chorus of the song, a tune so deeply ingrained in popular culture those around couldn't help but mouth along with the words they all knew:

"But I never meant to hurt you, and I hope that you can see, that I always thought I'd see you next to me...and the day I hope you listen is a day I hope I'll see, and I'll always keep it with me, preciously. Preciously..."

Tears rolled from Lorraine's eyes as the crowd sang with Rick, every word a chorus of sound around her head, her eyes fixed on Rick's as he sang the song to her, his eyes never wavering.

Finally, as he came to the end of the song Rick held the final note heroically until the crowd screamed with him, then thanked them as the applause died down. "Thank you very much, thank you, ladies and gentlemen of Mossy Grove. That means the world to me...but someone else here tonight means the world to me too." He set the guitar down and stepped from the stage, the crowd parting before him as he walked to Lorraine, no one daring to speak a word as the billionaire rockstar spoke in hushed tones to the woman he'd hurt so badly so many years before.

"Lorraine, I came here tonight because I hoped I'd have a chance to ask you to forgive me. Back then I was just a young, dumb kid who was afraid of losing his shot at fame, and I wasn't man enough to face you and explain why I did what I did. I don't know that it would have made any differ-ence, but every day since then, that decision has haunted me."

Her eyes brimmed with tears as he took her face in his hands.

"But worse, no matter where I've gone and what I've done, I've never been able to be truly happy because I knew deep down I'd hurt the only person in the world who really mattered to me--and I didn't think there was anything I could do to get her back."

Rick took both of Lorraine's hands in his own, looking deeply into her eyes.

"Lorraine, you'd make me the happiest man in the world if you would say you forgive me here tonight. If you can't, I understand--believe me, I understand--and I wouldn't blame you, frankly. If that's your decision, then I will never bother you again--and this will be the last time I come home to Mossy Grove as well, because seeing you this way stirs up too many emotions, and I--I..." Rick's voice choked with emotion. "I don't think I could take seeing you again, accidentally or otherwise."

Lorraine held the billionaire rockstar's calloused hands, still sweaty from the guitar cooling on the stage. She smiled, looking down at their fingers wrapped around each other for the first time in longer than she cared to remember. She raised her gaze to meet his dark eyes, and her mouth trembled.

"Rick, I...I want to forgive you, but this is just..." She looked around. "It's hard to think so...publicly."

He looked back at her softly. "I get you. But you'll...think about it?"

"I...I will, Rick."

He smiled. "Then that's all I can ask."

The crowd broke into excited whoops and cheers, and Lorraine smiled despite herself; Rick shrugged, the same way he used to when he thought he was getting away with something, and it was as though all the years of bad blood melted away in an instant.

The band started up again with an uptempo number and the party dissolved into small groups as Lorraine and Rick edged their way to the corner of the room. She smiled, realizing he was still holding her hand.

"That was quite a number you pulled there, Rick."

"Desperate times, desperate measures. I meant every word though, babe."

"And you still feel that way...seeing me now?" She bit her lip.

"No, seeing you now I feel more that way than ever before. You're just as amazingly beautiful as the day I first saw you, Lorraine--I'm just sorry I was so stupid to think we shouldn't be together because we were playing together, then stupid enough to think you'd be mad at me for breaking off on my own..."

"Oh, Rick--I didn't care which one of us it was in the spotlight--as long as we were working together. But when you weren't there anymore, I just didn't have it in me anymore."

"I know how you feel--for me it was the same, but opposite. All I've been able to do for the past ten years has been make music and make money. Oh sure, I'm good at it, and it's nice to be successful--but everything else in my life is a disaster. It's just one gig after another--without any light at the end of the tunnel, there's no hope waiting at the end of the road. The guys I play with, I see them aching for their families on tour and I feel empty--because I know I turned my back on my light."

She hugged him tightly to her. "Oh, Rick. I forgive you for everything you ever did. I hope we can start over from square one and rebuild our relationship."

"Well..." He smiled that devilish smile, and Lorraine felt herself fall in love with him all over again. "The hotel did provide me with the most luxurious suite available for the weekend. If you'd care to step away from the party with me for a moment..."

Lorraine took his hand. "Are you inviting me backstage, Mr. Rock Star?"

"I am indeed, young lady."

"Mmm. Well, I hope I won't be asked to do anything I can't tell my mother about."

"I guess that depends on what kind of relationship you have with your mother."

Up in Rick's hotel room, Lorraine felt as if she was dreaming. The huge suite was the largest in Mossy Grove but still maintained a certain indefinable homey charm that made her feel welcome and comfortable, even in the expansive living room.

Rick pulled a bottle from the brushed metal refrigerator, popped the cork and poured two glasses of champagne, setting the half-full bottle in an ice bucket to chill and handing one glass to Lorraine with a slightly chagrined look on his face. "Sorry about the room...I asked my manager to get me a normal one, but she always thinks I should play up to the billionaire rockstar image more than I'm usually comfortable with. Like that damn car this morning..." He shook his head ruefully. "God, I must have looked like such a jackass tearing up the road in that thing."

Lorraine grimaced sympathetically and diplomatically. "Well--it is a nice car."

"I tried to tell her that's not how people back in Mossy Grove do things, but I guess it went in one ear and right out the other." He met Lorraine's eyes and she felt a chill run through her spine. "That's why I need someone like you around to watch out for me." He held out his glass and clinked it against Lorraine's. "To us!"

"To...us," Lorraine echoed, sipping her drink and looking cockeyed at the handsome man. "What did you mean, someone like me?"

"You know, someone I can trust. Someone real, someone who really knows me--knows who I am, where I come from. This suite, that car--none of it feels comfortable or natural. I may have billions in the bank and a roster of hundreds on my payroll, but I'm still more comfortable behind the wheel of a pickup blasting old classic rock instead of hobnobbing in the hottest clubs with rail-thin starlets who are always checking their phones and ducking off into the bathroom for minutes at a time, coming back sniffing and rubbing their noses."

Her head spinning, Lorraine struggled to reorient herself. "Are you--are you making me an offer, here, Rick?"

Rick sipped the rest of his champagne and refilled their glasses, his face solemn. Setting the empty bottle in the trash, he looked Lorraine in the face. "Huh, you know--I guess I am. Look, I haven't really thought out all the specifics or particulars, but after tonight I have to leave immediately for a two week promotional tour--I'm going to be hitting all the major markets in a quick promotional blitz. Come with me, Lorraine--please say you'll come with me."

"Rick, I..." She bit her lip. "I have a life here in Mossy Grove. A job, an apartment--tempting as it may sound, I can't just drop everything and run away to join the circus."

"I know, and after all this time I wouldn't dare ask you to trust me enough for that--at least not yet." He put his hand to his chin thoughtfully. "How about this: if you have some vacation time saved up, you could come with me for a bit, see how the lifestyle works for you and find out if it's the kind of situation you might be interested in making more... ongoing. This way it's a win-win: you'll be able to test it out before making any drastic changes in your lifestyle, and I'll be able to show my manager what the perspective someone like you brings to the table can do for my career. What do you say?"

"It sounds pretty tempting, Rick--but I have one last reservation."

"What is it--salary, benefits, 401K vesting? We can match or beat whatever you need."

"No, it's nothing like that. It's--well, Rick, if we're going to be working together on a professional level, what about--us?"

"Oh, honey. Come here." He set his glass aside and hugged her to him; enveloped within his muscular arms, she felt small for the first time in recent memory. "Years ago I made the mistake of thinking that because you couldn't share a small part of my life, I couldn't have you in my life at all--and I've suffered all this time for that mistake." He cradled her chin and stared deep into her eyes. "No, I want you to be my other half in both my music and my life, Lorraine. I need you, and if you say no I don't know if I can keep going the way I have been--so please don't say no."

"Oh, Rick, of course I couldn't. This is everything I ever dreamed of, even if I wouldn't let myself believe it this morning."

She tilted her head back; he pressed his mouth against hers first lightly, then firmly as their lips parted and the two lovers tasted each other's tongues.

"Mmm..."

"Oh, god, Lorraine..."

"Oh, Rick..."

Rick's hand slid down the back of Lorraine's dress, finding the tiny zipper at the base of her spine holding it clasped shut. "I need to see you, Lorraine...I want to see all of you," he whispered, his voice husky from his earlier passionate vocal performance.

Lorraine looked around, blinking her eyes. "Isn't it a bit...bright in here?" She shivered.

"It's okay, baby, don't worry," His fingers tugged at her dress and she found it sliding from her body as his hands caressed her curves, his muscles against her soft skin driving her wild with desire. His eyes roamed up and down her curvaceous form and she saw his crotch rise with arousal, his prodigious endowment straining against the constriction of his tight, worn jeans.

"Oh, Rick--I can't stand to see you so uncomfortable," Lorraine gushed. She undid the snap at his waistband and the man gasped with relief as his pants loosed themselves; she slid her hands around his back and grasped his firm buttocks, pulling him against her firmly. She felt the tip of his erection pressing through his underwear against her stomach, and she smiled up at him.

He licked her neck delicately, nibbled her ear, and breathed, "You feel so good and soft, baby...I need to feel your sweet softness." He slid down her body, his hands caressing her as his lips nuzzled her ample cleavage, kissing her stomach as he moved down her torso, finally pressing his nose into the cleft of her already-damp panties.

She gasped, feeling her clit twitch at the pressure, "Ooh Rick, I want you so bad, baby. God..."

Kneeling at her feet, he smiled up at her. "I want you too, baby--I need to taste you now." He pushed her dripping panties aside, exposing her wet, warm labia. He pressed his lips against her softness and she felt herself gush deep inside, her vagina moister than it had been in years. His tongue parted her folds as he tasted her, groaning and taking her delicate wetness on his tongue as he gently caressed her, holding her body against his yearning mouth.

He found her clitoris and gently sucked her in and out between his lips. She felt her knees buckling and she gripped the back of his head with both hands, crying out as he tongued her slit, the man groaning with pleasure as he tasted her essence suffusing his senses.

"Oh, fuck, Rick, you are so goddamn good at that..."

He smiled. "Been dreaming about this for longer than you can imagine."

"Oh god, baby, I need you in me--I want you in me right now!"

Rick smiled and took her hand, helping her down to the floor as he leaned her back against the plush rug. He slid his already-stained boxers off, freeing his dripping member; Lorraine couldn't help but salivate at the sight of his throbbing cock, aching to take him deep inside her.

Rick cradled her head in his strong hands, staring down into her eyes, every fiber of his being glowing with love.

"I still can't believe you're here, Lorraine--this day has been like a beautiful dream."

"I know, Rick--I love you."

She clapped her hand to her mouth as she saw surprise spread on his face.

"Omigod, I can't believe I said that--it just slipped out!"

"It's okay, Lorraine, I'm glad it did--because I love you too, and I want you to know it. I want everyone to know it-- and soon they will."

He hugged her warmly and she embraced him, savoring his muscular form against her soft curves as they kissed deeply. Then she shifted her body, moving up against him until the head of his penis pressed up against her dripping opening.

He gasped as he felt her welcoming wetness on the head of his cock, then pushed his body into hers, his shaft sliding smoothly into her welcoming cavern. Lorraine sighed as she felt her body craving his presence sinking deeper and deeper into her, pulling him down upon her until she felt the full length of his massive cock sunk into her womb, pressing up against her cervix as she gasped with delight.

"Oh god, Rick--you're so big..."

"God, baby, your sweet pussy feels so good..." He slid himself in and out of her, the pressure of his throbbing shaft within her walls making her ache with delight as her flesh strained to accommodate him. He yanked her bra off in one swift motion and she squealed with pleasure, her sensitive nipples brushing against his hard chest as his body sank into hers again and again and again.

Lorraine felt her body rising to the heights of passion and she pulled him as deeply into him as he would go, savoring the sensation of Rick's thick cock contained within her body. She buried her face in his shoulder and gripped him tightly as she felt the orgasm rock her body, a wave of intensity that spread from her belly outward up through her fingertips and the top of her head, her entire body tingling with pleasure as she gasped his name.

"Oh god, Rick, Rick...oh my god, Rick..."

He smiled. "Wow, that was something else."

Lorraine gasped for breath. "Oh my god, baby, it was... and now, it's your turn."

"Do you want me to..."

She grabbed him by the neck and pulled him down to her, hissing in his ear. "I want you to come in me. I want to come in my pussy, Rick, I want to feel your hot seed deep in my belly."

He grinned and kissed her deeply. As his lips separated from hers she moaned, feeling him sink his length within her, his hands rubbing her skin as his dick sated its hunger within her warm opening. His rhythm escalated, his breathing faster and faster as he sank into her again and again, each thrust forcing the breath from her body in pants of pleasure and she smiled, knowing the greatest satisfaction she had ever experienced.

Finally, he convulsed and gripped her fiercely to him as his scrotum emptied its pearly payload, his spurting cock pumping Lorraine's womb full of his seed. She held him to her, feeling his massive member twitching within her body as the man groaned his pleasure for a full minute, his cock gushing load after load until his cum seeped out of her sweetly aching nether lips, dripping down her buttocks to the floor.

The lovers stayed silent, holding each other on the cooling hotel room floor, neither wanting to release the other. It had been too long, and too many years of loneliness to let go now.

They fell asleep that way, and as the reunion continued raging downstairs the two blissfully dozed the night away, smiles of deepest fulfillment emblazoned on their faces as they cradled each other--wrapped only in the thin hotel blanket, but warmed by the heat of love.

3
———

CLUB LUXURIA

Carl found himself on his hands and knees, every muscle in his body aching. He'd been out there digging for ninety minutes with barely a break before the man had relented and brought him back inside to clean himself up. The warm luxury of the shower was a blessed refreshment after hours in that empty field, but now he barely had strength left in his body to hold himself up-- every limb felt like limp spaghetti. Not that it mattered-- bound as he was, his head fully encased in a locked leather mask, he wasn't likely to be going anywhere anytime soon.

The room was eerily silent--almost as if it had been soundproofed, Carl surmised--and after the brutal physical exertion of his field excavation Carl couldn't help continually running over the details of his dilemma in his head. He'd missed meeting his contact out at the road--the roar of the passing 18-wheeler had told him that. Still, his supervisors had no reason to suspect he was in danger--and really, Carl wasn't sure whether he actually was. While admittedly it had startled him to hear the details of his life tumbling so casually from the man's lips, had they managed to discover that Carl was actually a federal agent sent undercover to investigate the goings-on at Club Luxuria he imagined that detail would most likely have gotten top billing.

He couldn't imagine they'd have allowed him to stay had they ferreted that fact out--but then, maybe they knew and simply didn't care. If they didn't have anything to hide, why *not* allow a federal agent to moonlight at the club? Certainly the pay was higher than anything he ever hoped to make in the government's employ--exponentially so--and years of service had sculpted his athletic body into a block of taut muscle. Perhaps everything at Club Luxuria was exactly as it appeared, as the man had laid it out for him both when he'd first interviewed and again back in that dark field.

Then again, in his years as a law enforcement official, how often was anything ever exactly as it seemed? He shook his head. *Damn, I'm really in a spot here.* He'd hoped to be in and out of the club before he was called upon to perform his duties, but if anything nefarious was taking place at Club Luxuria they had done a good job of keeping it well hidden. The good ones were always hard to take down, though--and Carl was a dedicated agent.

Nothing to do but bite my tongue, bide my time, and ride it out, he thought. *Best case scenario, everything is on the up and up, I do my job, go home and we get to pay off the house early. Worst case scenario...*he didn't want to think about it. And he knew that in any case, when things went bad you could never tell just how bad they were going to get--in Carl's experience, just when you thought you were about to hit bottom you often discovered new levels of the depths to which human beings would sink.

Just then he heard the door click open behind him and he focused his thoughts, memorizing every aspect of what he experienced. One never knew what would be the crucial piece of evidence, after all--Carl's job at that point was to be a human vacuum, taking in every aspect of everything around him, calling his attention to any detail that might indicate actionable offenses. More than once, the object of an investigation had unknowingly given the game away with a seemingly offhand aside in casual conversation--and if that happened, Carl wasn't going to miss a thing.

He flinched reflexively as the same voice that had rung out across the field now filled the room--though now its tone was laced with honey rather than steel.

"And here, sirs, we have your room for the evening. I believe you will find everything as you requested."

"It better be--we're paying enough for this one night, after all," a second voice grumbled.

"Oh honey, don't be a party pooper--it's not like we can't afford it a thousand times over. And I'm sure Club Luxuria's reputation wasn't earned by displeasing its clients, after all."

"That is correct, sir. And while I can certainly appreciate that our entrance fees are sizable, it's absolutely necessary. As well as helping restrict club access to only the world's most wealthy and powerful individuals, allowing them to satiate their every taboo desire, it's crucially important to maintain the standard of quality we provide--and to maintain our guests' complete privacy and discretion, of course."

"Of course. See honey, they have it all under control."

"They'd better--you know if our fans ever found out our tastes swing this way, our record sales would tank overnight."

Carl's ears perked up. Record sales? He hadn't realized Club Luxuria might have ties to the recording industry.

"I assure you, sirs, every aspect of your evening has been carefully considered and tailored to your exact specifications. To that end, I would like to introduce you two gentlemen to Jeffrey here on the floor."

"Hello, Jeffrey."

"Oh, Jeffrey won't be answering you at any point this evening--as requested."

"Good." Carl could almost hear the toothy grin in the man's resonant voice. "Thought I might catch you out trying to put one over on us there."

"Again, sir, while I can appreciate your caution, you will find it utterly unnecessary. All your specifications have been met down to the letter."

"You mean...?"

"Yes. Jeffrey here is a happily married, straight adult male with two children. He has never had a gay experience in his life of any kind--a fact we verified through extensive testing and background research. He is firmly bound here on the floor, and the mask covering his head obscures both his vision and his hearing--so while he is most likely aware someone has joined him in this room, he won't be able to make out any of what you say."

Carl's curiosity piqued; he wondered why the man was lying to the club's clientele--or if his ears had been left unplugged accidentally by the assistants charged with preparing him after his ordeal in the field.

"And I see he isn't wearing anything but that mask." The lust in the man's deep voice was palpable. "That's a tight-looking little virgin ass on him."

"I shall leave that to you gentlemen to determine. Is there anything else you require from me at this moment?"

"Nah--pour me a glass of that champagne and we're good."

Carl heard rustling, a pop, and fizzing as two glasses were decanted and distributed to the lustful men.

"Here you go, buddy."

"Sir, while I can appreciate the gesture, tipping is neither required nor allowed for employees here at Club Luxuria."

"That's a thousand dollar bill, sparky--just put it in your pocket and walk away, it'll be our little secret."

"Thank you sir, but no--above all other rules here at Luxuria, obedience to the rules is the one rule that must never be broken."

"Well--all right, your loss."

"And now, gentlemen, I shall take my leave of you-- simply press that red button on the console to summon me at any time, for any reason. Otherwise, you shall not be disturbed for the remainder of the night."

The door shut with a slam. Soon all Carl could hear was the sound of glasses clinking, then swallowing as the men gulped their champagne flutes.

"Aaah, that's good stuff--top quality."

"See, honey? I told you--the referral I got said Club Luxuria was the best in the nation. Maybe the world."

"It'd better be. I had to write three hit songs to make the money we're spending here tonight."

"Come here, grouchypuss." Carl heard kissing and heavy breathing, then rustling of clothes; the men seemed to have forgotten the bound, naked man on the floor beneath them as they groped each other.

"Oh baby, your hand still feels go good on my dick!"

"Like I told you all that time ago, it's the guitar that does it--after playing the axe all these years, I can play a hard cock like nobody's business."

"Yeah, well--for my money, the instrument you're most gifted at is the skin flute."

Carl heard a thump as the second man fell to his knees,

then a groan of delight and gurgling noises as he worked his partner's organ with his mouth.

"Oh fuck, baby, that feels so good--when we went into "Rockin' Town" tonight, I looked over and all I could think about was your sweet lips wrapped around my stiff dick."

Carl heard a gasp as the second man extracted his partner from his orifice. "Really? Cause I was thinking the same thing around that time." He gulped the hard penis into his throat and Carl heard a familiar tune as the man hummed away on his partner's throbbing dickhead.

"Ahh, that's the stuff. Man, those fans would shit themselves if we did this right onstage in front of them."

"That's...mmmph...that's why we come to places like this, remember?"

"You're right, come to think of it--after all, we can do this every night back in the dressing room. Come on--let's move on to the main event."

Carl could hear the wolflike lust in the man's husky voice, every syllable dripping with lascivious intent. Anticipation grew in the pit of his stomach, and he knew whatever happened, his life was about to change forever.

He felt a pressure on his face and experienced sudden blessed relief as the zipper over his mouth opened, releasing more sweet air into his lungs than the tiny nose holes cut into the mask had allowed him for the past several minutes. Carl gulped for air, his sore muscles still desperate for oxygen--but just as he started to inhale, a warm, fleshy presence suddenly protruded through the zipper, pushing between his lips and dripping onto his tongue--and his brain flared with revulsion as he realized for the first time in his life, another man's penis was in his mouth.

"Ohh, fuck," said the deep voice above him, pressing his shaft deeper into Carl's struggling throat. "Shit, that feels good...you know, now I don't think that dude was lying at all."

"No? How come?"

"Ah, fuck...you'll know the second you sink your dick into this straight little fuckpig's flesh. I can tell by the hot way his tongue is struggling against the head of my cock, the way his lips twist around me--it's nothing like what you do to me. You're my honey, but you're so gay sometimes it's like you love my cock too much."

"I can't be blamed for that! You have the thickest, hottest cock around!"

"Oh, now you're just being flattering. You know your cock is bigger than mine."

"Well, I can hardly suck my own dick--and believe me, I've certainly tried."

"I'm sure you have. But this guy, oh man--I can tell he's never had a dick inside his mouth before, so he doesn't know what to do or even how to breathe right. Check this out!" Carl felt a hand grip the back of his head and he felt his mouth being forced down on the man's huge pole; his throat contracted at the intrusion and he gagged, his esoph-agus violently trying to eject the massive object from his airway. Finally, the penis slid back out of him, air flooded back into his body, and he tasted the man's musky precum on his tongue.

"Shit, you're right--that guy's never even thought about deep-throating a monster like that in his life. Hey dummy, here's a helpful hint--breathe through your nose."

"Ahh...he can't hear you, remember? Can you, little fuckpig?" The man slammed the entirety of his stiff tool down Carl's throat at once, and he felt his straining gullet stretch to contain the man. "Jesus, that feels good. Come on, baby--you gotta get a piece of this too."

Carl winced--if the second man's cock was even bigger than this one, how would he ever keep it down? The first man kept sliding himself in and out between Carl's lips, tantalizingly close to full withdrawal from his weary mouth. The very second Carl would be sure he was going to remove himself, he'd jam his full length back down into him, making his throat ache with the strain. But if he wasn't going to share Carl's mouth, then...

Oh no.

Sure enough, as the first man once more rammed into his sore larynx, Carl felt a tickling against his backside--and his stomach withered in fear. The second man was definitely poking around down there; suddenly he felt a hand firmly grip his flaccid, dangling penis.

"Holy fuck, check this out--he wasn't lying! You've been facefucking this dude for a solid minute easy and his pecker's still limp!"

"Goddamn, you're right. He must really be as straight as they come--or he was until tonight. Come on, quit fucking around and help me spit-roast this little fuckpig."

Carl braced himself, or tried to--but nothing he could have done would have prepared him for the titanic intrusion he was about to experience.

First he felt the tip of the man's dripping head dancing around his tightly puckered hole, cinched shut as if hoping to remain inviolate. It was a vain hope, Carl realized, as the man's throbbing head found purchase, easing his anus open millimeter by millimeter as he wedged his glans into Carl's virgin behind.

"Ohhh, fuck, this is tight--so fucking sweet and tight."

"How far are you in?"

"I've only got the head inside--but it feels fucking amazing!"

Only the head? Carl thought, panicking. He already felt as if his ass was going to split open from the pain. The man eased back and forth with small motions, each maneuver edging his thick cock a little deeper into Carl's agonized rectum.

He'd almost forgotten about the thick cock still sunk in his throat, and was swiftly reminded as the two men began working at him in rhythm, the dick in his mouth pushing him further down on the one in his ass, the stiff member in his butt getting deeper and painfully deeper with each thrust.

Finally, the men clasped hands above him with a slap and pulled against each other with all their might. Carl felt his throat stretch wider than ever to accommodate the insistent penis lodged there, while his lower half exploded in blinding, burning torment as the second man's long, thick tool sank up to the hilt in Carl's flesh.

"Holy shiiiiit! Oh my god, this virgin asshole feels so tight and good against my hard fucking cock!" The giant organ tore in and out of Carl's body hungrily, giving no thought to the delicate tissues tearing in its wake. Carl yearned for the time only minutes before when only one thick dick had punished his body; as the two men insatiably pounded into him, he felt as though he might black out or go irretrievably insane.

Suddenly, the dick in his throat paused. "Jesus Christ, look at that!"

For a blessed moment, the cock in Carl's ass halted its intrusion, still lodged deep in his inflamed pipe. "What? What?"

"There--look at his fucking dick!"

Suddenly Carl realized with horror that without his

knowledge and against his will, his penis had risen to a state of full arousal.

"Holy shit--I think we literally fucked this guy gay!"

The men high-fived over his back--while inside, Carl agonized. *How can this be?*

His mind was a maelstrom of turmoil, but he had barely a moment to process his confusion before the two merciless dicks resumed their assault, even harder and faster than before--but now, the man with his cock in Carl's ass was also reaching around to stroke Carl's hard cock as they moved. With each motion, Carl's body racked with the pain of being violated by two massive pricks shoving mercilessly into him for the first time in his life --and worse, now the agony was tinged with the thrill of delight for Carl's penis, inarguably responsive to the rapturous joy each stroke delivered.

"Hey, the little fuckpig's starting to like it--you were right!"

"Come on baby, I'm starting to get there. Move with me-- let's blow this guy's straight little mind once and for all."

The two men moved as one, almost as if their two thick penises were appendages of one monster also expertly working Carl's twitching, throbbing dick. The man's fingers danced expertly along the ridges and veins of Carl's pulsing member, and Carl shuddered inside as he realized he, too, was on the edge of explosive orgasm.

Groaning in unison, the two men working Carl's shattered body suddenly broke rhythm and rammed into him as deeply as they could, simultaneously bellowing their bliss as their stiff members twitched furiously, pumping both Carl's throat and rectum full of hot, spurting cum--as Carl's scrotum also released its load, spilling his tortured seed across the carpet, his brain exploding in joy but racked with confusion.

Sighing, the two men finally removed their satiated members from Carl's aching body--though not before Carl had swallowed the load bursting from his lip, the other man's semen dripping out of his stretched anus and down his freshly relieved ballsack--and he breathed deeply as his tortured flesh began to return to its natural state.

Just as he began to relax, the first man's deep, commanding voice rang out again and Carl cringed again with anticipation. "Jesus, that was good...pour me another glass of that champagne, will you? After all, it's early yet... and we have the use of this room and our newly gay little friend here all night long.

HOURS LATER, AFTER HIS TWO "GUESTS" had departed, their needs thoroughly sated, Carl lay huddled in the corner of the tiny room. The events of that evening rolled through his head as if on an endless loop while Carl struggled to process what had happened. A titanic wave of emotions had battered his psyche in ways he hadn't been fully prepared for, even with the mental conditioning and endurance techniques he'd been taught.

No matter what, now I have *to stay*, he thought. *No matter what I have to endure from this point forward, I'm going to get to the bottom of whatever's going on here at Club Luxuria...or lose myself trying.*

4

TRUE LIVES OF MILITARY WIVES

I n my role as a U.S. Military emotional counselor, I treat all kinds of psychological issues ranging from post-traumatic stress disorder to shell shock to drug addiction--yet even I still get taken off guard by the shockingly depraved sexual behavior exhibited by many military wives today. I was trained not to judge the patient and to dissociate the person from their actions, but when I hear about--and sometimes see--the things that these military wives today get up to, I don't mind telling you, it can turn one's stomach.

Why, just this week I had a military wife come in for counseling here on the base--we have an open door walk in policy for any member of the armed forces or their families at any time. To look at her, anyone would think this woman was the stereotypical perfect military wife--at her man's side, looking lovingly up to him, keeping in constant contact, always supportive of her husband--basically, exhibiting exactly the kind of behavior we like to see in the warfighter's familial support system.

However in this case--typical of many of the types of

cases I see in military wives today--her husband had deployed only the week before and already she was tortured by unfulfilled taboo sexual desires. Of course, while her husband had been home they'd had regular relations, but typically, her description of these encounters made them sound fairly routine and forgettable. Though she expressed nothing but love, attraction and desire for her husband, the patient's tone of voice sounded somewhat bored as she unenthusiastically described her loyal husband's hard member pushing into her--though it sounds like their love-making was satisfactory by most standards. Yet when this patient began describing her sexual thoughts and behaviors since her husband had flown back overseas, both the tone of her behavior and her voice changed, getting deeper and darker.

That first night after he was redeployed, she put on a trench coat and an oversized pair of glasses and visited several area strip clubs. Why the trench coat I don't know--I suppose it to be a subconscious dissociation of identity, though she claimed it was an attempt at disguise. That night, all the patient did was go from one strip club to the next, sit quietly in the back, sip her drinks, and watch the dancing of the exotic young ladies onstage--as well as the behavior of the horny clientele. Afterwards, she went back to her empty home to sleep alone next to her husband's framed picture by the bed.

But the next night....well, I don't mind telling you that some people today have differing ideas of homosexual behavior. I tend to take a clinical view based on medical training, where I see it as symptomatic of underlying psychological issues--in this case, separation anxiety coupled with abandonment issues and unfulfilled reproduc-tive urges. But if you could have heard the tone in this woman's voice when she was telling me about her behavior....though her words were all about how regretful and ashamed of her behavior she was, berating herself for her weaknesses--her tone was that of sensual delight and deep fulfillment.

She had risen that morning as she always did, getting up earlier than most people in order to chat via webcam with her deployed husband off in a foreign land due to the eleven-hour time difference. She claimed that they had a good chat, that they didn't argue or give any indication that anything might have been amiss--and yet the very second she was finished chatting with her spouse, she was on her phone calling a friend of hers.

This friend was also a military wife whose husband was a friend of the family; the two men had come up through the ranks together and trusted each other like brothers. As a result, their wives had come to be close acquaintances and frequent social companions, though they came from exceedingly different cultural backgrounds. My patient was originally from a small Midwestern farm town, while the other woman had a more sophisticated, urban upbringing--yet the commonalities of the military life, always trailing along in their husbands' wake as they traversed the globe, had brought the two women together on multiple occasions.

My patient didn't indicate any nefarious intent or hidden agendas when she'd called her friend over that morning, intending only to share a glass of wine and share her stories of the previous night's adventures before planning on heading out to the farmer's market--and yet, I can't help but think some part of her had premeditated the entire course of events. Because when I analyze her actions, I can't help the conclusion that every choice she made pushed the day's actions in a certain, very specific direction--so either she is a very, very good liar seeking absolution for her sins, or her subconscious has been shaping the direction of her life in ways even she is not aware of.

First, of course, there is the decision to greet her friend and begin their morning with a glass of wine. As it did in this case, one glass often leads to two, and drinking first thing in the day can often be an indicator of deeper issues--not that we need such indication in this case, as those issues obviously came bursting into the open with full force.

After wrapping up their idle discussion regarding the events of the day, my patient--let's call her Cindy for the purposes of this discussion--had cleared her throat, looked the other woman deep in the eyes, and asked her, "Have you ever been to a strip club?"

Despite her urbane background, apparently this other woman--who my patient called Cherise--nearly choked on her chardonnay at the question from her young friend, whom she had always thought of as untouched and naïve due to her Bible-belt upbringing.

"I have, once or twice," she said. "Back in college, on a dare. Have you?"

"Not until last night."

"Ooh, you naughty girl. Do tell!"

"Well, I was feeling lonely, the way I always do when the boys leave--but instead of curling up with a steamy book the way I usually do, I put on a coat and glasses and went out."

"By yourself? Girl, you should have called me!"

"I know. I thought of it afterwards. But right then, I didn't know if I was really going to go myself. Honestly, I figured I'd get up to the door and chicken out, turn right around, and come home..."

"But you didn't?"

She shook her head. "No, I didn't. No, I paid my admission and walked right in, sat in the back and watched the girls dance. And then I went to another club and did the same thing, and then another one...it was like I was in a trance the whole night. I just kept staring at these young girls, so brazenly displaying their most intimate places for the pleasure of any paying customer...and the whole time, the same thoughts kept running around in my mind."

Cherise laughed. "Girl, you aren't thinking about getting a side job, are you? Cause you know we're holding together pretty good, but I don't know if either of us is strip club quality."

She shook her head. "That's just the thing, Cherise--I kept looking at these women, and I realized that they're all different. You'd think there's just one type of stripper girl, but there isn't. It's a crazy variety out there, all these different types of girls, and in each club an entirely different group. And all any man--anyone--has to do to see their goodies is walk up and pay admission."

"It's a story as old as time, hon. As long as there have been people, there have been those willing to pay other people to get a peek at their naughty bits--or more than that. That's why they call hooking the oldest profession, after all." She looked sharply at her friend. "You're not thinking of hooking either, are you? 'Cause I hear that a lot of dancers do that too--but it can be dangerous. Real dangerous."

"No, I don't want to do that--but, um...the thing I kept thinking of all night was, I wanted to go up and ask one of the dancers if she...did that."

Cherise's eyes widened. "You don't mean...?"

"I guess I was thinking it'd be a safe way to, you know... try it out. With a professional, someone who knows how to be discreet. But I kept looking at these girls, and I couldn't decide who to talk to, and I was afraid I'd get kicked out if I asked wrong...I mean, it was all I could do to work up the strength even to go into these places. So I kept going from place to place, telling myself I'd ask a girl at the next one, but then the next thing I knew it was closing time."

"Did you ever...?"

"No." She lowered her eyes to the table. "I never could work up the courage, and all of a sudden I was back on the street, alone. By then I was pretty drunk, so I got a car home, and well, here I am." She tilted her glass. "Hair of the dog that bit me."

"Well, you probably did the right thing."

"How's that?"

"I used to know a lot of the girls who worked the clubs, and yeah, some of them go both ways, but mostly it's just gay for pay. You know? It's basically anything for pay with some of them--and sure, that might have been fine, but Cin--do you really want your first lesbian experience to be with someone who's just biting her lip and getting through it for the money?"

"First lesbi...?" Cindy trailed off.

"That's what you're talking about here, isn't it?"

"I...guess I didn't really think of it that way. I was just following my...compulsions. But do you think I'm really a..."

"Lesbian?" Cherise laughed. "Girl, you could be anything from A to Z. There's a lot more in this world than just straight and gay. A lot of these macho dudes you see macking on the hottest babes on the planet have also taken thick cocks up their backsides."

Cindy blushed. "Cherise!"

"Well, it's true. And a lot of the time it's just a question of availability: you put a dude somewhere without women for long enough--like prison--and he'll let another guy go down on him pretty quickly. And after that, it's a slippery slope--you know what guys are like. A wet hole is a wet hole."

"You don't think...I mean, what about our husbands over there?"

Cherise looked thoughtfully at her friend. "Hon, I wish I could tell you. We're in the same position military wives have been in since the dawn of civilization; we only know what our husbands and their superiors choose to tell us. We know a lot of our guys left babies over there in Southeast Asia back in the day, sure--but where our guys are, I don't know what the prospects are. I don't think they can just duck out to a brothel. So who knows? Maybe they're sucking each other off right now!"

"Cherise!" Cindy slapped her friend's hand playfully. "You're so naughty!"

Cherise shrugged. "Look, soldiers are practical men by default. They know they have certain needs to be met, and they're trained to fulfil those needs in the simplest, most direct way possible so they can get back on the front lines. And you know our guys have been together for a long time, Cin--can you really tell me you can't picture it?"

Cindy thought hard, trying to imagine it. True, their husbands did hang out a lot, both in and out of uniform--and sure, they did seem to slap each other's butts when they played sports--but more than that? She tried to picture her husband taking Cherise's husband's penis in his mouth, or jerking his buddy off. She wasn't sure whether the image fit the facts she knew about the man she'd been married to for years--but she knew thinking about it made her horny.

"I--guess I can sort of see it."

"Sure. It's just real life, hon--people have urges, and they need their urges met."

"So--what about me? What about my urges?"

Cherise smiled. "Well, Cin--you never did really tell me what it was you actually wanted to do with those stripper girls."

Cindy's cheeks reddened. "Oh, I don't know myself, really--I guess I figured, you know, they'd know what to do and show me."

"Hey, Cin--there's no need to be embarrassed." She placed her hand over her friend's and squeezed it gently. "Just relax and think back. What were you picturing when you were looking at those young girls? Think about one of them that really leaped out at you--what was going through your mind when you were looking at her?"

Cindy recalled that there had been one girl at the third club she'd attended, large breasted and wide-hipped with a tiny hourglass waist and a leonine head of tawny hair she swung around expertly, entrancing all within sight with the rhythm of her sway. Cindy had nearly convinced herself to talk to the curvaceous girl after her set, but got distracted when the next girl came on brandishing a tennis racket--and then the next thing she knew, the tawny girl had vanished. But if she was honest with herself and she had been able to entice the tawny girl into coming back to her place, she would have loved to rub her face on those firm, round bosoms, pull the taut young girl's body to her, and plunge her fingers inside the young girl's shaved crotch. And after that...she shuddered. Who knew?

"Well...honestly, I think the thing that kept me from ever going up and asking any of them was I kept thinking--they don't know me or anything about me, really, so how are they going to know what pleases me? I mean, we've been together for years, and my husband sure doesn't--oop!" She turned red and clapped her hand to her mouth. "A couple of glasses of wine and I start running off at the mouth!"

"Oh, girl--it sounds like you just haven't been getting what you need for a long time. It's no wonder you're going a little crazy--if any of us don't get our rocks off for long enough, we start losing it. And from what I can tell, you need to get yours off in the worst way."

Cindy cried. "Oh god, it's true!" Tears streamed down her face. "I'm just so fucking horny! I feel so weak--why can't I resist my urges?"

"Hey, hey--come here." Cherise embraced the emotional young woman, taking her into her arms and pulling her to her, compassionately patting her on the back as she cradled her head on her shoulder. "You're no weaker than anyone else, Cin. You just haven't learned to handle it yet."

Cindy pulled away from Cherise's shoulder and look into her eyes, both women brimming with emotion. "So teach me to handle it like you do, Cherise--please, please teach me!"

Cherise kissed Cindy on the lips and suddenly they were one, their tongues dancing against each other as the women explored the deepest corners of each other's mouths. Cherise reached around the small of Cindy's back, pulling her torso to her as their full breasts pushed against each other, all four of their nipples erect. She slid her hand down and grabbed Cindy's tight ass, squeezing hard enough to make Cindy yelp slightly.

"Hey!"

Cherise slapped Cindy's firm buttcheek. "Oh, don't lie--you know you like it."

Cindy smiled. She *did* like it--and this was what had been missing last night. If only she had realized it then: what she needed was a trusted friend, someone who knew her inside and out, someone who knew what she'd like--and could show her.

Cindy bent over before her friend. "Please--won't you teach me more?"

Cherise smiled and wound up her arm. "All right--but this one's gonna sting!"

She spanked Cindy's wanton ass and her friend squealed with delight at the impact. "Ooh, Cherise...I can feel my pussy starting to get wet already!"

"Well, girl--if that's what you like, then let's see how much you love it." She grabbed her friend's head and pulled Cindy to her, kissing her deeply as her other hand slid down to the waistband of the inexperienced woman's pants, loosing them and sending them tumbling to the floor.

Suddenly, Cindy found herself bent over her friend's lap, her bare buttocks pointing skyward, only the thin thong underwear standing between her bare skin and Cherise's raised hand. "Ooh, Cherise--are you going to punish me?"

"You've been a naughty girl, Cindy--such a naughty girl that I don't see that I have any other choice." She lifted her hand as high as it would go, then brought it down on her friend's bare backside with all the strength in her body. It hit with a loud smack and Cindy screamed with the impact, the red imprint of Cherise's hand clearly visible on her left buttock.

"Oh my fucking God! Oh my god!"

Cherise only smiled and slowly lifted her hand again, this time bringing it down on Cindy's right buttock with even more force. She screeched as the swift hand whacked her tender buttocks, forcing tears to her eyes from the pain...but as it cleared, she found her mind filled with a joy she had never known before.

"Holy god, Cherise--feel my panties!"

Cherise placed her hand on the cleft between her

friend's legs; sure enough, they were soaked through, dripping with Cindy's juices.

"Damn, girl--you're wetter than a Portland summer." She held her hand against the thin cloth covering Cindy's opening, then started rubbing in a circular motion, spreading Cindy's lubrication throughout her pussy as Cindy pushed back against her friend's expert hand.

"Ooh, fuck--your hand feels so good..."

"You like that, huh? Do you want more?"

"Oh yes, Cherise...please, put your fingers in me!"

Cherise smiled and pulled Cindy's sopping panties from her, exposing her swollen labia; she gazed lovingly at her friend's tender opening, aching to taste her sweet essence... but not yet.

Gingerly, she parted Cindy's quivering nether lips and slid one thin finger into Cindy's yearning canal; the untested young woman moaned at the touch. "More, please...I want to feel more of you inside me!"

Carefully, Cherise added a second finger inside Cindy's tight slit, then a third, twisting her fingers within the squirming woman bent across her lap, fingering her sensitive g-spot and rubbing her clit with her thumb. "How do you like that, hon?"

"Oh fuck, your fingers feel so good--oh yes, right there, when you touch me like that it drives me crazy--you feel so good, but I still need more of you inside me!"

"I don't know girl...are you sure?"

"Please, Cherise--please don't torture me! Please tell me you'll give me more!"

Cherise smiled. "Alright girl, but just remember--you asked for this." Removing her thumb from Cindy's clit, she carefully slid her little finger alongside her ring finger.

Cindy writhed on her lap in ecstasy as she wriggled her fingers, driving the young woman wild with joy.

Finally, she added her thumb, until all five fingers on her hand were ensconced within Cindy's aching cavern.

"Fffffuuuuuuuckkk," Cindy hissed. "Fffffuuuuckkk, that feels so tight and good!" She pushed back against her friend's hand, sinking her deeper into her, and she shouted with delight.

"Is this what you needed, Cindy?"

"Yes, oh yes, Cherise!" She bucked on her friend's lap, the other woman's hand sunk into her vagina deeper than her husband had been in years. "Please, Cherise--please fuck me!"

Cherise took a deep breath. "Alright, girl--just try to relax." Slowly, she eased her hand further and further up Cindy's birth canal, until she was sunk into her friend's pussy up to her wrist. "You still okay?"

"Fuck yes, bitch--I'm better than I've ever been in my life!" She moaned and pushed back against Cherise's hand. "But I'm still just on the edge of orgasm--can you give me just a little bit more?"

"More, girl? Are you sure you're ready for that?"

"Please, Cherise--I'm begging you, please Cherise, please fuck me harder, please fuck me more!"

Deep inside Cindy, Cherise balled her hand into a fist, causing Cindy's womb to contract around her.

"Oh, fuck," Cindy gasped.

"Fuck indeed," Cherise agreed. "You wanted to get fucked? Well, you're fucked now."

Slowly, Cherise began sliding her balled-up fist in and out of Cindy's strained pussy.

"Oh my fucking God, Cherise--your fist is like the cock I always needed inside me but I never knew it until this moment! Oh my fucking God, I feel like I'm going to tear apart--but please, don't stop, don't ever stop!"

Cherise's pitiless hand rammed into her friend's aching vagina over and over, forcing tears of joy and pain to both women's eyes, until Cindy felt a spark open inside her and her body was racked with waves of intense orgasm, far stronger than anything she'd felt before. Gushers of clear, sweet girl cum came spurting out around the edges of Cherise's fist buried tightly within Cindy's birth canal, soaking the two women as Cindy bellowed her climactic bliss.

"Oh, fuck, oh my fucking God, baby...that was so fucking good! After that, how will I even be able to feel my husband's little cock inside me at all?" Still bent over her friend's lap, she looked back over her shoulder up at Cherise. "God damn, hon--you knew exactly what I needed!"

Cherise smiled. "Yeah, I've been thinking about it for a long time, actually--I couldn't wait for you to get around to the same conclusion!"

Cindy blushed. "Well I didn't know. Is this what all military wives get up to when their husbands aren't around?"

"Well, I can't speak for all of them...but around here, pretty much everybody I know has a kink or three."

Cindy smiled. "A few days ago I might have disagreed with you...but now I guess I can't deny it." She looked at her friend. "But I just realized--you just got me off, and I haven't done anything for you! What's your kink, baby?"

Cherise just looked at her. "Haven't you guessed? Here-- give me your hand." Cherise pressed Cindy's hand to her crotch; it was, if anything, even wetter than Cindy's own. Cindy's eyes widened with the shock.

"You mean, you came...just from giving me pleasure?"

"Only three times." She leered at the young woman. "But the day is young yet."

The two women smiled knowingly at each other, both anticipating the day yet to come and the many hours to be filled with forbidden carnal pleasures until their husbands eventually returned from deployment--neither noticing the little red light on Cindy's webcam or the still-active signal she'd been sending continuously for the past hour, while her astonished husband watched from the other side of the world.

5

TAKEN RAW

As Kenny wiped down the gym mats, he cursed the coach for the hundredth time.

So what I didn't have the right clothes today, big deal...it's not like playing volleyball in street shoes is really gonna tear up the gym floor. Besides, the coach always seemed to have something against Kenny and always had, through all four years of his high school education. Kenny guessed it had something to do with the fact that he was tall, lean, and muscular, and looked just the type to fill one of the many gaping holes on the Mossy Grove varsity basketball team-- but unfortunately, Kenny lacked the coordination necessary to take advantage of his height. The first couple of years, the coach would drill him relentlessly in class after class, trying to instill some sense of the fundamentals into the boy, but by the time Kenny was a junior his fate was sealed--no matter how he tried, the coach wasn't able to teach him to be an athlete.

Since then, gym class had been a never-ending litany of barely-veiled contempt, the aging gym teacher desperate to live out his declining years vicariously through the victories of boys on the verge of becoming men, yet somehow always blaming Kenny for his own inability to inspire greatness from his students. Kenny wiped the sweat from his brow as his reflection glared back at him from the locker room wall. *Old prick is too afraid to face his own damn self and his failures,* Kenny thought.

Behind him, the locker room door banged open and a hulking figure brushed into the room, casually tossing a red and blue gym bag on the floor. Kenny's head jerked instinctively and he kicked into defensive mode; he'd been stuck at the school too many late afternoons not to know how to handle unexpected visitors.

"Hey, school's done for the day, buddy--if you're looking for your kid, they're probably out front."

The large man looked cockeyed at the young boy. "Sorry, I'm not here picking up." He held out his massive right hand to Kenny: "Hi, I'm Travis--Travis Hardesty."

Kenny felt his jaw drop. "No way--the same Travis Hardesty who was voted offensive player of the year three years running?!"

Hardesty shrugged. "So they tell me. I just try to keep my head down as much as possible and do my best to keep myself at the top of my game--which is why I'm back here in the old high school gym while I'm back here visiting."

"Really--you work out here?"

"It's a constant battle to stay on top, son," the older man lamented. "You like football when you were a kid? 'Course you did. You're old enough now to have seen some of those guys who were your heroes age out of the game--how they holding up?"

"Well..." Kenny thought about the interview he'd seen with Robbie McGarson the previous weekend. McGarson had only retired from the league two years before, but he'd evidently spent every waking moment since then eating chicken wings and guzzling beer.

"Yeah. So you see my point--sure, it's nice to get awards, but winning games is what keeps me employed. And the only way I know to win games is to make sure I'm always at my best, and the only way to do that is hitting the gym every day, without fail."

"Jeez--you really do every single day?"

"Every day, without fail--Christmas and my birthday not excluded. The only time I missed was that time my ankle was whacked out for a few weeks a couple years ago--and if you recall, the team lost every damn game without me."

"Haha, yeah--my dad was pissed. He lost a bunch of money betting on those games."

"Serves him right--betting on football is a sucker's game. Putting in the work day after day is the only way to get ahead in this life, son--I try to live my life following that example, and I credit that with everything I've been able to accomplish. Sure, I've been blessed--but I've worked damn hard to get where I'm at, too. Here, feel that--there's your proof."

He flexed his massive arm, holding it out for the boy to feel his bicep. Kenny ran his fingers over the thick, ropy knot of muscle, and his eyes bulged in appreciation of the older man's body.

"Wow--that's something else!" He smiled at Hardesty, but suddenly his expression fell and his eyes sank to the ground. "Still, even if I worked out like you every day of my life, I'd never be able to accomplish a tenth of what you have."

Travis placed his muscular hand comfortingly on the younger boy's shoulder. "Well, I might be able to show you a few things while I'm here--what position do you play?"

"Ah, I'm not even on the team--I mean, Coach hates me,

but it's not like he's wrong. I'm just not any good. I mean, sure, I have the right build for it--all the girls always think I'm an athlete when they meet me--but I just don't have the coordination, or my balance is off, or something, 'cause I just can't play any sports for crap."

The older man winced. "Ouch. Well, I'm not gonna lie--being good at sports has been pretty good to me. Over the years, it's opened a lot of doors...along with other things. But you know, football isn't for everybody--in fact, sports in general is really only for a very, very small number of people. The number of great high school players who never play college is brutal, the number of college players who never play pro worse. And then even if you get to the big game, there's no guarantee you're going to stick around... anything can happen at any time. No matter where I am, on the field or off, I'm always only one bad step away from ending my career forever."

"Geez, I never thought of it like that."

"Sure. That's part of why I try to always be my best, to live every moment to its fullest, and to savor the fruits of my victories--because you only go around once, right?"

"Right, but...well, if sports isn't my thing, my grades aren't much better either."

Travis clapped Kenny on the arm. "Look, I know when you're at this time of your life, things can seem overwhelming--what are you, 17?"

"18 last month."

"There you go. When you're 18, the world seems big, scary, and overwhelming--I know it did to me, and I always had football to help me out. But the truth is, all these adults out there who seem like they have it all figured out? Inside every one of them is a scared little kid, just terrified of being found out."

Kenny's eyes widened. "Really?"

Travis smiled warmly. "Really. We're all just trying to muddle by in life, and I get how to a guy like you it might seem like I have it all together with my championship rings, endorsement deals, billions of dollars in liquid assets--but even I have my demons. None of us get through this life unscathed, after all."

"I guess you're right. It's all so confusing, though--I just wish I had someone to talk to about this kind of thing. It's nice to hear someone else has the same feelings I do."

"Well, what about those girls you mentioned earlier? Whether or not they think you're an athlete, if they're talking to you that's a good sign."

"Uh...nah," the young boy flushed. "I mean, I've had a couple girlfriends, but it...hasn't really worked out."

"Well, son, don't worry--it takes a long time to find that right someone you can spend your life with. I mean, look at me--I'm 28 and I still haven't!"

"It's not that, so much. It's..." The boy looked around furtively. "I mean, when I made out with them, when they put their hands and stuff on my thing, I didn't....feel the way I was supposed to."

"You mean you haven't..."

"No, I haven't ever. Not much of anything, to tell the truth. I mean, I liked these girls, you know? They were all really pretty, and they all tried really hard...but no matter what they did, I just could never get..."

"Hard?"

The boy blushed. "Yeah. So ever since then I've been worried something was wrong with me. I mean, they did everything they were supposed to, I did everything I was supposed to--it's just not fair. Why does everything have to be so difficult?"

"Well--here, sit down." The older man patted a spot on the locker room bench. "Things aren't necessarily as hard as they seem. Sometimes it helps to break things down and look at them logically. Okay, so you're not good at sports or girls--but there are lots of other things to do in this world. So you failed at a couple of things, big whoop--I fail all the time, but what's most important is that you get back up and keep going."

"B-but, well, what if I'm, you know...gay?"

The older man smiled. "Well, Kenny, being gay isn't the worst thing in the world. Sure, you might have to dance around some intrusive questions about your personal life now and then, but as long as you remember that your personal life is just that--personal--most of the time, things are okay."

"Y-you mean you're..."

"Gay? Sure. I mean, don't go running around telling everyone, but there are a lot of us in the league--it's just not, um, popular among everyone in the audience, so we're encouraged to keep it on the downlow."

"When did you first realize you were gay?"

"You know, now that I think about it, it was a time a lot like this. I was a young man myself, getting scouted out by the best colleges in the nation, all wanting me to come play for them--only this one scout, he really just wanted me to come for him. And boy, did I."

Kenny's cheeks reddened again. "W-wow."

"It really wasn't such a big thing--actually, it was a big thing, but I mean it wasn't so different from a million similar things that happen every day." He scooted closer to Kenny on the worn wooden bench, until their thighs just touched. "Like I said, we're all just trying to find our way in this world.

And sometimes, you find someone who's willing to help you find your way."

Kenny looked up at the powerful older man shyly. "Mr. Hardesty...do you think you could be that someone for me?"

Travis smiled. "Kenny, I was starting to think you'd never ask."

He stepped over to the locker room door and snapped the lock shut, a lupine grin spreading across his face.

"Okay, Kenny, we'll take things slowly--if I do anything you're not comfortable with at any time, be sure to tell me, okay? You won't hurt my feelings, and after all, we're doing this for your benefit. Sound good?"

"Okay." Kenny felt nervous--butterflies were turning over in his stomach, but he trusted the powerful older man.

"Alright." Travis sat back down on the bench and gently cupped the young boy's head in his powerful hands--hands that had driven their hometown high school's team to two state championships. He tilted the boy's head back, parted his lips, and pressed his mouth to Kenny's. The boy jumped at the shock, surprised at the gentleness of the huge man's soft kiss, and he dared to dart his tongue into Travis's mouth.

Travis smiled. "Ah, you like that, eh? Okay." He ran one meaty finger up and down the front of Kenny's torso, feeling the ridges of his young chest, stroking the contours of the boy's body. "How does that feel?"

"F-feels good...but I bet yours feels better." Kenny reached out to the wealthy football player, his eyes widening as his hands rubbed across Travis's massive pectorals. "Wow, that's...w-wow."

"You like my muscles, Kenny?"

"I really do."

"Then let's get you a closer look." The man pulled his

thin t-shirt up and over his head, smiling as he tossed it aside. "Here, let me help you out of that," he said, reaching for the edge of Kenny's green MOSSY GROVE H.S. gym uniform shirt.

As Kenny felt the shirt pull free of his body, he breathed deeply and saw the older man's eyes hungrily scan his form. "Do you...like how I look?"

"I like how you look, Kenny--I like it a lot. Come here." The men embraced, pressing their naked chests together, reveling in the warmth of each other's bodies, their tongues dancing in each other's mouth and their hands exploring their bodies, one hulking and muscular, the other slender and smooth.

"Mmm, this feels so good, Travis."

"Better than with those girls you tried with?"

"Oh yes, " Kenny gasped. "So much better."

"Let me see." Travis reached his hand down to Kenny's thigh, resting it a moment and feeling the beat of the boy's heart in his firm upper leg muscle before sliding it up slowly towards Kenny's crotch. The young boy inhaled sharply as the older man's probing fingers found the waistband of his worn gym shorts, pulling them away from his body and slipping inside. "Oh yes, Kenny...it seems we have signs of life down here after all."

Kenny gasped as the rich football player grasped his young virgin cock firmly, squeezing his shaft as he kissed the boy's neck, licking the delicate beads of sweet young sweat dripping down his cheek. "Jesus, Travis, that's...really something..."

"You think that's something? Then you'll really like this!" Suddenly, Hardesty dove down on the young boy's cock in one swift motion; before he knew what was happening, Kenny felt his pulsing dick encased in the powerful man's mouth, so surprisingly delicate in his touch. Travis's hand grasped at Kenny's balls while he slid Kenny's length in and out between his lips, savoring the taste of young boy precum against his tongue.

Kenny moaned in ecstasy, his young dick harder and more aroused than it ever had been in his life before. Howling, he grabbed at the older man's broad back as he suddenly came a gusher of cum into the football player's throat, his scrotum pumping his sweet load from his spurting member as Travis smiled, Kenny's dick still between his lips as he licked away errant drops of the boy's cum.

"You were backed up, huh?"

"Oh my god...I'm sorry I came so fast, Mr. Hardesty!"

"Don't be silly, Kenny--after all, if I hadn't wanted you to come in my mouth, I wouldn't have been working your balls like that. There's nothing to be sorry about--the only thing you need to worry about is whether you're enjoying your-self. And are you?"

Kenny smiled broadly. "Oh, yes."

"Then everything's fine. Now, you'll probably need a few minutes to recover--but you're young, you'll be ready to go again in no time. In the meantime, do you think you're ready to try returning the favor?"

Kenny looked down at the football player's prodigious crotch, wondering at the size of what might be within those nondescript gray gym shorts. His eyes widened, and Travis saw excitement and a little fear there.

"I-I'd like to, but I've never, um..."

"Don't worry, Kenny--we'll take it slow." Travis pushed a single meaty thumb between the boy's lips, rubbing it on his tongue. "Here--do you like the way that feels?"

Kenny sucked lightly on the man's digit, rubbing his

tongue along the ridges of the man's fingernail. "That doesn't seem so bad."

"Well, I'm not going to say a cock is the same thing--but if you can suck a thumb, sucking a dick isn't too much different." The pro athlete stood before Kenny and dropped his gym shorts to the floor, exposing his rapidly rising member; Kenny's eyes goggled at the sight of the alpha male's elephantine penis.

"W-wow. I've never seen one up close in person before--other than my own, of course." Suddenly, he looked at the older man fearfully. "A-are they all this big?"

"Haha, no--I wish, " Travis laughed. "No, I'm quite lucky--especially in my line of work, where a lot of guys aren't nearly as big as people think, sadly. Stay away from steroids, kid--they'll wither your balls, and your cream is too sweet to waste like that."

"Th-thanks, I will." He was fascinated by the sight of the muscular football player's thick cock, easily ten inches long already and continuing to rise beneath his gaze. *How could anyone ever manage to take something like this up...you know?*

Travis smiled down at the young man, seemingly hypnotized by his gargantuan penis. "Don't worry, Kenny--it's not as intimidating as it might seem. Just take it slow, enjoy yourself, and no matter what remember everything is all okay."

Tentatively, Kenny opened his mouth and slipped the head of Travis' pulsing cock between his lips. The older man groaned above him, savoring the feel of the boy's tender flesh on his hungry rod, resisting the urge to grab Kenny's skull and force his length down the young boy's virgin throat. Instead he simply relaxed as the untested young boy explored his body, taking first an inch, then two inches into his mouth while he gently fingered Travis's dangling scrotum.

Kenny slipped the huge erect cock from his mouth and smiled up at the football hero above him. "Tastes really good. Like musky, salty...something or other. I can't place it, it's on the tip of my tongue..."

"It sure is, Kenny. I'm glad you like the taste. Do you want to try more?"

"I do. I really, really, do." He grasped the huge dick eagerly and swallowed as much of the star's aching organ down his throat as he could, desperately forcing the giant shaft into his stretching orifice as he yearned to feel as much as possible of the man inside him. First he was only able to get a few inches inside his mouth, his tongue anxiously licking away the tasty precum leaking from the tip before again straining to fit more inside his gullet. Travis gasped as the young boy hungrily gobbled his member, astonished as the boy sank nearly the entire length into his esophagus before coughing, his tortured passage violently ejecting the huge intrusion as Kenny sputtered, his face reddening.

"I-I'm sorry, I tried to fit it all down my throat, but I couldn't get that last inch--it's just so big!"

"Hey, Kenny, don't worry--you were doing great there!"

"R-really? You mean it?"

"Definitely! I really should have stopped you, honestly, but I was shocked at how much you were able to keep down for so long! And your tight little mouth just felt so good on my cock, well...you shouldn't feel bad at all. That's honestly the best blowjob I've had in a long time--most guys can't keep half that much of me down!"

"Thanks, Travis, that means a lot, but well...I wasn't embarrassed because I had to choke, I actually felt more disappointed in myself. Because I wanted more than anything to take all of that magnificent cock inside myself--but I just didn't have the room there."

"Well, Kenny, if that's really what you want there's only one way to really go about it--but I can't tell you if you're ready for that. Only you can decide that for yourself. I certainly have my preferences, of course, but I'll respect your choices."

The older man stared hungrily at the young boy's lithe, slender form. He prayed Kenny would allow him to get up inside that tight virgin asshole, and the alpha male billionaire desperately fought his aggressive instincts telling him to overpower the smaller man and take what he wanted, right there on the locker room floor whether he wanted it or not--but he shook his head, driving the thoughts from his mind. No, beyond the simple fact that it was the right thing to do, a sudden accusation of sexual assault had derailed many an athletic career and lost many an endorsement in the past--and Travis was simply too smart to allow himself to be overpowered by his hunger.

But oh, that ass, he thought, gazing wistfully at the untouched boy's pale buttocks. *It would almost be worth it.*

Finally, Kenny took his thumb out from between his teeth and turned to address the hulking, muscular athlete. "I want to do it," he said. "I want you to fuck me."

"You're sure about this, Kenny?"

"Yes. I want you to put that hard dick inside me and fuck me until you cum all up inside," Kenny said. "It's time for me to step up and take it like a man."

Travis smiled. "I'm glad you made the right decision, Kenny."

"Don't thank me--just get over here and put that dick inside me before I start getting second thoughts."

Travis didn't have to be told twice. He turned Kenny

around and rubbed his tight young buttocks warmly, feeling the boy's taut skin against his rough, calloused hands. Suddenly, he pulled his hand back and slapped the boy's ass, just hard enough to leave the outline of a red handprint in his wake.

"Oooh, that stings!" Kenny said, smiling.

"This'll help warm you up," Travis intoned, his voice deep and resonant. He fingered Kenny's tight, puckered asshole, pushing the tip of his finger inside and feeling the untouched sphincter grip him anxiously. He could tell the boy hadn't been lying; no ass this tight could ever have had anything up inside it before.

He withdrew his finger and turned the boy around, bending him over the locker room bench as he braced for entry. Travis's prickhead found Kenny's tiny starfish and the boy whimpered in anticipation; Travis rubbed the precum dripping from his cock around the tight bunghole, providing at least a modicum of wetness to help ease Kenny's transition into adulthood.

Taking a deep breath, the giant man eased the tip of his colossal dick into Kenny's rectum. The boy moaned low and deep at the feel of another man's organ inside his ass for the very first time, and he pressed back against the bench, sinking another full inch of the huge dick into himself. The insistent pressure made him gasp, and Travis patted his back reassuringly.

"It's okay, there's no rush...just let yourself relax into it." The boy's tight asshole felt so good clenched around his throbbing dick, he worried he'd cum too soon if the boy went too fast.

"No, I w-want to...it feels so good deep in my butt, I need to feel you deeper inside me!" He thrust himself backwards and howled with pain as the giant dick sank another couple of inches into his racked behind--and yet, he'd still only managed to take half of the giant cock so far. Travis closed his eyes in ecstasy as the boy's ripped orifice struggled to contain him, his young tissues unprepared for an assault of such titanic proportions.

Kenny breathed deeply, bracing himself, his tortured insides slowly acclimating to the insistent presence of the older man's massive, erect cock in his colon.

"You okay, buddy?"

"F-fuck yeah, I'm okay...god, your giant cock feels so good filling me up, I can't believe I've lived this long without it..."

Kenny opened his eyes and stared across the locker room, spotting their reflection in a mirror mounted on the opposite wall. He smiled at the sight of the famous billion-aire athlete hunched over him, all attention from the massive hulking form concentrated downward at the lithe young body encasing him--his body.

My body, Kenny thought. *This is me. This is who I am, and this is what I want to do in life.*

Suddenly, with all the force in his body he pushed back against the locker room bench, forcing the entirety of the older man's huge cock inside his rectum at once. He screamed first with agony, then with joy as a triumphant grin spread across his face--*I did it!* He smiled back over his shoulder at the man buried inside him up to the hilt. "I got you all inside me!"

"F-fuck yeah, you did, kid...fuck yeah, you did!" The foot-ball hero's brain was a riot of joy as the full length of his member felt the pleasure of the young boy's flesh, gripping him tighter than anything he could remember in his life. He gripped Kenny's hips and the two moved together as Travis grunted his pleasure, ramming himself in and out of

Kenny's ass, each thrust forcing a smile to break across the boy's face as the enormous dick stretched him further and further.

At this point, the wealthy athlete could stand it no more: his massive arms grabbed Kenny with both hands and he shoved him down onto the bench, driving his giant cock into the boy's aching ass over and over and over, faster and faster as the powerful man approached the height of pleasure. His thick, ropy muscles held Kenny firm against the bench as he fucked him again and again, changing the topography of the boy's insides in ways that ensured he would never be the same again.

Finally, he pulled Kenny's ass tightly to him, driving his full length further inside the boy than ever before as he reached explosive orgasm, shooting gallons of cum into Kenny's shattered colon. The football player stayed hunched inside the boy for a full minute, each twitch of his scrotum pumping more spurting hot spunk inside him until it gushed out around the torn remains of Kenny's anus still desperately gripping the shaft of the older man's still-erect dick, dripping onto the cement locker room floor beneath them.

Kenny smiled, clenching his buttocks as the giant man's satiated member slid from his inflamed backside. "I did it," he muttered, almost as if in disbelief. "I did it!"

"You...you sure did, kid." He patted the boy in victory, then hugged him to his broad chest. "You okay?"

"Better than that--I think I may have found the thing I'm actually good at."

"You might be right at that, kid, you might just be right. I gotta admit, I mainly got into this to try and help you through a rough time...but that was the hottest lay I've had in I don't know how long."

"Really, you mean it?"

"Really. In fact, I'm going to be back here to work out tomorrow around the same time--like I say, I never miss a day--and if we run into each other again, maybe I can offer you a few more tips. Or, hell, at this rate maybe you can offer me some."

"I'll be here. In fact, I don't know if I can wait that long!"

"Well, kid, this seems like it might be the beginning of a beautiful friendship. And who knows--maybe you aren't good at football, but considering the talent you've shown me here today, I might just have to take you on the road with me!"

Kenny grinned at the thought of it, the opportunity to pleasure the powerful man, coming again and again inside him, filling him up with his essence--and he knew that no matter what the coach had to say to him tomorrow, he'd never pay attention to the old bastard's harsh words ever again.

6

WHEN DADDY'S AWAY: OLDER MAN YOUNGER VIRGIN WOMAN ROMANCE

Will Wainwright and I walked in silence through the decaying corridors for a hundred yards or so. Though the grounds had been kept attentively swept—but not vacuumed, I noticed—each item of décor we passed struck me as more decrepit than the last. Granted, were the facility to have been kept open for business during the intervening years it would undoubtedly have been renovated, restored, and rejuvenated with modern conveniences, perhaps several times over.

Then, too, I surmised such fripperies were not likely valued highly within Will Wainwright's culture. The gruesome scars of many amateurish repairs paid mute witness to his people's attempts to address problems well outside the scope of their abilities; their rudimentary handiwork had clearly been performed to the height of their knowledge yet still fell far short, utterly devoid of the care and attention that had been lavished upon every inch of the structure by the master craftsmen who had originally constructed the building. The overall effect, then, was that of a once-luxurious palace of indulgence which, over a period of decades, had been converted into a ramshackle fortress of banal practicality.

Reaching the opposite end of the building, Will Wainwright ushered me through a darkened doorway into a musty concrete stairwell. As I mounted the staircase, I reflected upon the multiple cobweb-encrusted elevators we had passed along our path; all had appeared long disused and presumably nonfunctional—quite understandably, as I imagined qualified elevator maintenance and repair services must be difficult to secure in such an isolated community.

Upon reaching the structure's topmost floor, we exited into a narrow gaslamp-lined corridor. Though the well-worn carpeting we trod was identical to that on the ground level, other details indicated third-floor residents likely enjoyed an elevated level of luxury: the quizzical sigil pinned to my breast had been intricately carved into the surface of each door, handwoven doormats depicting elaborate designs were precisely placed before every threshold, and carts of the sort typically used for delivering room service awaited collection outside more chambers than not, each laden with a number of covered serving trays.

Arriving at the end of the hallway, Will Wainwright unlocked a door bearing an immense sigil hewn across much of its surface area and swung it open with no small degree of ceremony.

"My quarters are as yours, Carson Adkins," he offered as we passed through a surprisingly roomy foyer lined with mirrors. "I hope you will find them to your liking."

I concede I was struck by the sheer size of his living space. The rooms he occupied must once have constituted one of the resort's finer suites, consisting of a cavernous living room, a smallish kitchen, and no less than three separate bedrooms. Evidently, Will Wainwright's status within their society came with its perks, though based on his actions so far I had no reason to doubt he'd earned them.

"Father!" A young woman burst from the second bedroom and fairly leaped into his arms, embracing him warmly. "What are you doing home so soon?"

"Ah, Savannah. As always, it is pleasing indeed to once again gaze upon your lovely countenance. But regarding the reason for my early return: may I present Mister Carson Adkins?"

Dislodging her arms from around his neck, she extended a lithe hand out towards me. Smiling crisply, I shook it and enunciated, "Happy to make your acquaintance," as pleasantly as I could manage. As her father had declared, she was indeed a lovely young lady, eighteen or nineteen years of age, with dusty brown, shoulder-length hair framing narrow eyes, an aquiline nose, and full, bowed lips.

She returned my smile shyly, then glanced to her father. "An outlander? This is a surprise indeed. Wherever did you come upon him?"

"Wandering through the catacombs, attempting to find his bearings. He'd ended up just outside the nursery chamber, of all locations."

"It is good fortune that my father came upon you, Carson Adkins," Savannah declared. "Many would likely not have proven so forgiving of your unfamiliarity with the homestead, and instead leaped to the assumption that you might have intended the young ones harm."

"I can imagine," I answered—though at that time, of course, I could only guess as to what depths she hinted.

"It should have been clear to any with eyes to see that

this man was not placed among us with nefarious intentions," Will Wainwright protested. "And you must concede that even if he had planned maltreatment of the young, he could scarcely have done much worse than others who claim to follow the guidance of received wisdom."

I squinted at him. "What do you mean?"

"Nothing of import," he replied, waving me off.

Before I could press for elaboration, a knock on the door interrupted our conversation.

"Excuse my rudeness," Will Wainwright said, already striding back towards the front door.

Leaning in conspiratorially, Savannah lowered her voice to a whisper. "Father feels the homestead's traditional methods of child rearing to be overly harsh, but cannot declare so openly."

I was pleased to find my new companions evidently shared my low opinion of their nursery's quality of care, though the revelation only pollinated my mind with an abundance of fresh questions.

Mindful of my circumstances, I chose my words carefully. "Were you subjected to such a...traditional upbringing?" I asked.

Savannah shook her head. "My mother raised me in isolation, far from these walls. For this reason some think me weak, less blessed than those who claim to be true sons and daughters of the homestead. Were it not for Father, I might be considered fit only for positions of service, assuming I was not banished outright. Fortunately, thanks to his station he managed to persuade the council that my mother acted alone, of her own volition, that neither he nor I should be made to suffer the consequences of her actions, and that I deserved the same protection any other member of our society merits."

"How did he do that?" I asked.

"By convincing them that not only did he have no hand in her choices or my upbringing, but that he was prevented from doing so—because until the moment only two years ago when I was delivered to the walls of the homestead, he was unaware he had a daughter at all."

"Good lord," I gulped.

"So they say," Savannah muttered.

A host of queries flooded my mind, but Will Wainwright rejoined us just at that moment. "My apologies, Carson Adkins, but it seems a matter has arisen which requires my presence. Sadly, I must beg off sharing a table with you for the moment—though in any case, as my skilled daughter would also have prepared any food we might have consumed together, all you shall truly be deprived of is whatever poor company and conversation I might have offered. I am confident that by leaving you in Savannah's capable care, ultimately you will find yourself more entertained and enlightened than you would have had I remained."

I looked back and forth between man and girl. "Are you sure you're comfortable with this? You did just meet me today, after all. I could hardly blame you for not wanting to leave a stranger—and one from 'beyond', at that—alone with your teenage daughter."

He looked as though struggling to repress a smirk. "To you, my daughter may seem delicate," he replied. "However, those lucky enough to enjoy the pleasure of her company tend to learn quickly that her willowy exterior hides a heart of iron. As well, I never claimed you would be left alone."

Placing two fingers between his teeth, he whistled loudly. Within a heartbeat, a monstrous beast bounded into the room and leapt upon him, causing Will Wainwright to fall to the floor struggling with the mammoth creature. I clutched for my rifle momentarily before noticing the unmistakable sound of raucous laughter emanating from the scuffle while Savannah looked lovingly down at the brouhaha.

"This brute is called Leto," Will Wainwright gasped, attempting to regain his footing as the thing continued pawing at him. "A more loyal companion neither man nor woman could ever find. Leto, this is Carson Adkins, a man from beyond. I would ask you to guard him as you would myself, Savannah, or any of our own."

Never having been an aficionado of dog breeding or animal husbandry, I could only guess at Leto's parentage. The animal appeared undeniably wolflike, though much larger than any wolf I was aware of—likely outweighing me by a good ten or twenty pounds—not to mention friendlier, at least among those he trusted. I surmised that Leto was likely some sort of wolf-dog hybrid; perhaps his ancestors had been interbred with Great Danes, English mastiffs, or other large dog breeds to eventually produce this impressive beast.

Leto eyed me up and down; I decided instantly that I would do whatever might prove necessary to stay in the animal's good graces. Will Wainwright scratched the dog's ears, grinning. "Between Savannah and Leto, I trust you will be well cared for in my absence, Carson Adkins. If I might offer one final piece of advice before taking my leave of your company, may I suggest you take this opportunity to recuperate as fully as possible from the ordeal you have so recently endured? I know not how life is paced in your world, but within ours I have found such moments of respite to be rare indeed."

"Thanks, Will Wainwright. I'll do that."

"See that you do," he replied, turning to his daughter. "As to you, Savannah, I would impress upon you the fact that this man has traveled a very, very long distance to be among us. As such, he is not accustomed to our ways. Therefore, think not poorly of him should his manner of bearing not be as you might expect; instead, let us remember that all bear the marks of the environment of their upbringing, for which they are not to be held accountable, and it is in the strength of our choices that one's true character is demonstrated, not our inculcated attitudes."

She bowed her head. "Yes, father."

"I shall return as soon as I am able. Until then, I wish you well, Carson Adkins," he intoned, grasping and shaking my hand firmly.

"Same to you," I replied.

"I need no such wishes, though the meaning in your intent is accepted. Rather, those who stand against me should hope their loved ones have sent them the best of wishes. They are far more likely to find them necessary."

He winked and his daughter giggled. I gathered that was what constituted a joke in their culture and suddenly wished I'd downloaded more comedy podcasts onto my phone when I'd had the chance.

Immediately after the slamming of the front door heralded Will Wainwright's exit, the walls seemed to close in around me. I felt more out of sorts and self-conscious than I could possibly have imagined. What was I doing here? How had I ended up here in the first place? In that moment, it all seemed so overwhelming, and I despaired of ever feeling normal again.

Conversely, Leto apparently had no trouble at all acclimating himself to my presence, having curled into a huge furry ball on a mat in the corner, seemingly oblivious to the world around him.

"May I fetch you something to drink, Carson Adkins?" asked Savannah breezily.

"Uh, sure," I answered, suddenly all too aware how long it had been since the water I'd packed for yesterday's hike had run out. "I can't deny I'd love a beer, if you have one, but literally anything would be fantastic right now."

"I am afraid spirits and the like are prohibited within the walls of the compound. I can but offer the juice of the apple, tea, and the waters of the blessed spring."

"Apple juice sounds great."

She returned clutching two mugs of juice and handed one over. "To new friends, new worlds, and new life," she declared, raising her mug.

I repeated her oath, tapped my mug to hers, and took a hearty sip. "Delicious," I professed, and while I would likely have said so in any event, I meant it: after one sip, I truly felt as though I had tasted apple juice for the first time in my life, every liquid under that appellation I had previously consumed now a pale substitute for the platonic ideal I savored.

"Why, thank you, Carson Adkins. It was produced only this morn."

"Just Carson is fine, thanks. Or Mr. Adkins, if you prefer; I notice your society seems big on formality."

"It is," she sighed. "The Wainwright traditions hold iron-clad sway here—hence the aforementioned proscription on alcoholic beverages, as well as other sense-addling ingredients."

I made a mental note to keep the nature of my intended cash crop to myself when future recountings of the circumstances of my arrival in their society proved necessary before commenting, "Does that work? Back where I come from, we have entire counties that try to keep alcohol out, and from what I understand most of those places have horrible meth problems."

"Meth?" The tone of innocence in her voice was almost heartbreaking.

"Crystal methamphetamine. It's a nasty drug, used mostly by people who have given up on life. If you've lived this long without encountering it, consider yourself lucky."

"Oh, I do, Carson Adkins, every day. Have you ever used this meth?"

I considered my reply carefully before replying, "No, never. And I told you it's okay to call me Carson."

"I am glad to hear you are not the type to give up on life, Carson." She smiled and drained the remainder of her mug. "Have you finished your juice?"

"I have, thanks," I answered, handing the empty cup back to her. "Best I've had in my life, no exaggeration."

I thought I noticed her blush slightly as she accepted the returned mug. "Your compliments are accepted graciously, unnecessary though they are," she called out as she trotted back into the kitchen. "Now, if you would disrobe and lie down, I can commence the rejuvenation of your body in earnest."

I was thankful to have already finished my juice; were I to have had a mouthful at that moment, I surely would have spit it out in shock at her words. As it was, I scarcely managed to choke out a barely coherent "Wh-what?"

"Father said you had traveled far, yes? Do you not generally find yourself in need of replenishment at a long journey's conclusion?" She was rubbing her hands together as she reentered the room. "A deep massage is necessary to work free the many small inconveniences the body accumulates through the indignities travel forces upon us. This shall be followed by a heated soak in the waters of the blessed spring, during which I shall occupy myself preparing this evening's meal, including all the appropriate herbs to supply your body the tools it shall require to rebuild itself during your subsequent slumber."

I glanced over at Leto, still curled inert in its corner. "Are you sure your father would approve?"

Her head cocked to the side. "Why would he not? You heard his directive with your own ears, did you not?"

"Well, sure, but...where I come from, if a guy left his friend alone with his teenage daughter, then came back to find him, er, disrobed, in his daughter's company, the friend would be likely to find himself jumping out the window in a hurry."

Savannah giggled. "That will not be necessary. First, I would advise you that a leap from the height of these windows would almost certainly prove fatal even to the most skilled of acrobats. Second, my father has trained me well, and therefore trusts that my abilities more than suffice to care for all within his quarters in his absence—my own self included.

She smiled indulgently. "I am sure that in time you will have the opportunity to demonstrate your virility."

"That's...quite an enlightened view for such a young girl, Savannah."

She peered at me. "I am beginning to grasp just what a distance you have traveled to land among us, Carson Adkins."

I shook my head. "One last time: Carson is fine."

"Carson." She smiled shyly and indicated a comfortable-looking mat on the floor. "Shall we begin, Carson?"

I take her face in both hands, tilt it upwards to meet the light, lean in and kiss her firmly, holding my lips pressed against hers for just a few seconds. After releasing her, I turn away as if ashamed of myself: "I'm sorry, I don't know what came over me. I shouldn't have done that."

"No, it's okay...really."

"Really? But I don't want to pressure you into anything...."

"Just....wait there a second." She stands up and my eyes hungrily scan her firm young body from head to foot. She rapidly locks the door, then turns back toward me, smiles and unbuttons her jeans slowly, revealing her swollen virgin mound straining against cool white panties, already damp with flecks of her passion. Sensuous beyond her years, she slides her jeans slowly off her slender, coltish legs, kicking them off her tiny feet one at a time, finally dropping them on the floor beside me. Crouching down upon her pants, she hugs me hungrily to her, pushing the flannel off my shoulders onto the floor behind me, places her luscious pink lips next to my ear and whispers, "I want this to happen, I need you more than anything. But I just...just have to tell you this one thing..."

I pull away from her, suddenly serious. "What is it, honey?" She looks down, and I look down with her, entranced by her untouched slit, outlined clearly even in the shaded valley of her crotch as her pure sweet juices soak through the thin fabric.

"It's just...see, I just turned eighteen last week, and I..."

"It's okay, baby, you can tell me anything." I smile warmly.

"Well, I never...had...a man before." She blinks those big green eyes, looking up at me so beautiful and innocent. "So...um...can you just, be...gentle with me?"

She smiles shyly, trembling slightly, suddenly aware of herself sitting half clothed on a strange bathroom floor.

"Oh, honey. Thank god you told me ahead of time. Of course I promise I'll do everything I can to make this nice, slow and easy for you."

She smiles, all her fears assuaged, and moves herself closer to me. I stand until the crotch of my pants is level with her head; catching my intention, she grins devilishly and looses the belt of my pants, unzipping the fly and whipping my hard cock out in her comparatively tiny hand. Surprise and a flicker of fear swim across her face—clearly my endowment is more than she was expecting—but her rising passion soon overcomes any hesitation, as her untamed sexuality guides her into womanhood by instinctual patterns so deeply ingrained they seem carved by the hand of God.

Tentatively, she takes the head of my massive, pulsing cock into her mouth, at first unsure but taking to it rapidly. In moments she's sliding her lips up and down my length as if she'd never tasted anything quite so delicious and fulfilling in her life, my precum already leaking down into her throat and dripping off her lips as she forces her head further and further down on my dick. Even I had to give it to her, she was motivated: I don't think I've ever seen a girl take so enthusiastically to sucking cock as if she was born to it.

I let her continue for a few minutes, in my bliss as an untouched eighteen year old girl worked my throbbing cock with every fiber of her being, so anxious to please, to start her womanhood out right, to prove she can handle what it takes to be a real woman.

I smile kindly and gently into her wide, innocent eyes looking up at me hungrily, wanting nothing more than the validation of knowing her lips wrapped around my dick make me happy. In those moments, I loved her purely and without restraint, for I saw into her soul—and the light I saw there still warms me today.

I cup her face gently with one hand, lean back until my head nearly topples me backwards, and moan: "Oh my Christ, that feels so good, so good, so goddamn good, oh god...oh god, you have to stop that, you have to stop now."

She smiles up at me and removes herself from my cock, giving one last lick up its entire length, as if leery to give up the taste of my essence soaking into her willing mouth. Understanding my intent, she reaches down and helps me step out of my pants—first one leg, then the other—then she maneuvers my cock back through the fly of my boxers and pulls them off me, until I stand before her naked.

I sit on the floor before her, lean over, and gently pull her shirt up and over her head; she reaches behind her back to unlatch her bra, and shows me the most exquisitely untouched pair of perky young tits imaginable. No cum had ever splashed these tits, no cock had squeezed between them, not even the hand of a man had so much as brushed against them in passion before.

I stretch my legs out straight and beckon her forward onto me. She slides herself forward, wrapping her legs around my torso, pressing her feather-soft tits against my waiting lips, licking and nibbling as she rises to my touch.

I slide one hand around her smooth body, cupping the lumbar roll at the small of her spine, and slide the other hand over her impossibly unmarked thigh, up the inside of her leg, and finally to her warm, welcoming crotch.

I let my fingers linger at the waistline of her panties for a moment as though to slide them off her, but instead I simply push them aside, pulling her down until the head of my cock—dripping with precum, glistening with her own saliva

—pushes against her anxious, trembling pussylips. I let it dance around the edge of her tiny pussy, making doubly sure I'm lined up right, as the tiny slit between her legs makes for a challenging target—and for what I have planned, I need to get it right the first time.

Finally certain I'm set properly, I ease the first tiny fraction of an inch of my cockhead into her untouched cunt. I barely get anything inside when I hear her whimper and she clings to my body for life, knowing everything is about to change forever for her.

I take a second to relish the moment, then take a deep breath with all the strength I possess I pull her all the way down onto me, forcing the entire length of my steel hard dick deep into her unprepared body with one unforgiving motion. She cries out in surprise and pain as my hungry cock tears through her maidenhead in one pitiless thrust, leaving her forever rent in its wake. I feel myself deep inside her body, past where any wetness had prepared her for my entry—and I exult as her young cunt remolds itself, reshaping in the mold of my cock, turning her body from a girl's into that of a woman, once and forever.

At first, of course, the shock of forcing the entirety of my prodigious manhood inside her tight pussy has her thrown, but after a moment as her insides remold themselves in the wake of my invading intrusion, she begins to push herself into me further and further. Relishing the feel of my cock driving into her more and more until she catches up my rhythm and moves with me, first with tentative motions but soon riding me fiercely, bucking like a cowgirl, thrusting my cock deeper and deeper, tearing into her again and again, building and building until she suddenly grips my chest with both hands, drawing blood as her nails dig into me, out of control with orgasmic joy. She throws her head back, her blonde hair flying like a halo, cumming for the first time with a pure joy like nothing she'd felt before, and the image is something I'll relish forever: her body now limp with pleasure, feeing the true ecstasy only a woman knows rolling through her body for the first time, caressing herself in delight, writhing on my cock as her bliss spread across her face in the biggest smile shed ever given.

"Oh my god," she muttered again and again, "Oh my god oh my god oh my god." She shudders and clings to me as all the muscles in her body relax and she collapses forward onto my chest, her arms clasped around my neck for support. "I'm...so happy," she said. "Just so happy with your cock filling me up. But I didn't feel you, um...I mean, did you..."

I smile indulgently. "Not yet. But if you're happy, well...I guess that makes it my turn."

I pulled her down onto my hard, hungry cock and shifted my weight forward, lying her back against the cool bathroom tile floor. Now fully prepared, I lowered myself back onto her, pinning her to the floor with the weight of my body as my hard penis reentered her dripping pussy, already looking quite different than it had when I'd first slid those panties aside.

I pressed my mouth against hers, and she hungrily swallowed my tongue, thrusting hers into my mouth as if to crawl inside me once and forever. I put my hands on each of her shoulders and pulled myself into her as deep as I could; another explosion of pain flashed across her eyes as she felt my cock sink even deeper into her, changing the architecture of her insides with every jab.

I pushed myself into that warm wet cunt again and again and again, stabbing deep into her womb mercilessly, each plunge forcing a whimper from her lips as she felt my throbbing dick ram into her sopping wet pussy, irreversibly stretching her flesh beyond anything it had ever felt or even dreamed of before.

Finally I felt myself approaching the height of pleasure. I grabbed her by the head and I stared deep into her eyes, watching with ultimate pleasure as the hard truth of womanhood finally sank into her, imprinting itself on her soul as a lesson she would never forget.

The moment I saw that realization enter her, I knew her transition was complete: she would truly never be a girl again. The knowledge thrilled me, and my joyful cock grew another quarter inch in response.

Knowing the end was near, I marshaled the last of my energy for three final pushes.

Once: she cries out, wrapping herself around me, feeling a deeper pain than any she'd known before, but still needing me as if she could imagine nothing worse than having to remove my cock from her pussy.

Twice: my cock pushes even deeper into her, meeting something resisting its entry, and I feel a twinge of pain in the head of my cock. I know this is it, and I prepare myself to relish this joy.

Three: with all the strength left in my body, I force myself as deeply as it will go; inside her, I feel whatever resisted my last entry give way as her body reshapes itself one last time. Sunk as deeply into her as anything has ever been or ever could be, I let loose a bellow of animal proportions as my cock finally gives up its payload, filling every nook and cranny of her insides with my hot white spurting cum. I'm so fucking hot that I cum into her for a solid minute, each throb of my satisfied dick pumping her battered pussy with more of my seed—until finally, I'm drained and she's overflowing with my essence.

Dazed but deliriously happy, she smiles up at me and tightens herself on my cock, making more of our combined juices spurt out and leak down her ass, seeping out into a mess of blood and cum on the tiled floor as my satiated dick finally slides out of her. I hear her breathily sigh. "Thank you. Oh god, thank god, thank you. I never knew it would be…like that."

I brush the hair from her face and smile down at her. "I'm glad you enjoyed it."

After the sight of the girl's countenance returned my bearings to me anew, she led me into the bathroom, wherein I found a freshly drawn, steaming bath waiting for me in a long, clawfooted tub draped with fresh linens. I confess I found its waters so comforting that I scarcely managed to wash myself clean before feeling myself succumbing once more to the temptation to alight on the shores of Morpheus; despite a distinct and off-putting metallic scent, the waters proved so marvelously adept at relaxing my musculature that upon extracting myself from them, wrapping myself in her father's spare robe and sitting down for dinner, I felt as tranquil and serene as if I had been in my own comfortable, familiar surroundings back at home.

Dinner itself was comprised of humble but nourishing fare of the sort I imagined had likely been prepared in the area for hundreds if not thousands of years, consisting of a hearty stew of potatoes, carrots, and some mixture of game meats I thought likely to include rabbit and deer, though I refrained from questioning my hostess too closely regarding the dish. Having already demonstrated my utter lack of eminence in tactical offensive skills, I thought it better to avoid the potential for further offense to her sensibilities by reacting in an untoward manner to named ingredients I might be unfamiliar with. Better, I thought, simply to relish its delectable flavor without lifting the curtain of its precise composition; occasionally, I suppose, the common saying regarding the condition of ignorance presaging a state of bliss may bear some truth.

In any case, the meal settled well in my stomach, and presently upon finishing the final spoonful I again felt the tendrils of slumber touching at the corners of my mind. Savannah, again anticipating my needs, had already made up the spare bedroom and provided an appropriate-sized set of flannel bedclothes for me to wear, whisking my filthy garments away and promising to have them washed and replaced before I awoke.

As Savannah extinguished the bedroom lamp and closed the door behind her, the reality of my circumstances sank in with such gravity that I felt my mind reeling at the enormity of it all. It was too much for one mind to bear so quickly; I half-expected to close my eyes and awake in some utterly alien environment, as if transported to another planet entirely or unwittingly abducted in my sleep. My surroundings combined with the bizarre circumstances of my arrival defied credulity as it was, though in the dim light I could readily imagine the rich and entitled of a hundred years ago luxuriating in these same chambers, pampered and attended to by armies of servants rather than one eighteen year-old girl. It was almost comforting to imagine myself in their place, soothing my path toward sleep with the fantasy I was an entitled dandy from years past enjoying a restful getaway in my family's favorite mountain resort, away from the chatter and clamor of telegraphs, radios, motorcars, and the like which infested the cities of that day.

Despite having been delivered by a solitary eighteen year-old girl, it was undeniable that the recuperative routine administered by Savannah had proven strikingly effective.

Thus stretched out, wrapped in exquisitely comfortable bedclothes, imagining myself as someone else entirely, I don't mind admitting that within moments, I was deep in the arms of a dark, dreamless slumber.

THE END